A NOVEL

HENRY FRANKS

Peter Adam Salomon

flux™
Woodbury, Minnesota

First Edition
First Printing, 2012

Book design by Bob Gaul
Cover design by Lisa Novak
Cover art: Grunge floral frame: © javarman/Veer
Photo © Alex Stoddard
Interior Art: Chapter art © Llewellyn art department
Newspaper tears © iStockphoto.com/Mehmet Ali Cida

Flux, an imprint of Llewellyn Worldwide Ltd.

Library of Congress Cataloging-in-Publication Data
Salomon, Peter Adam.
Henry Franks: a novel/Peter Adam Salomon.—1st ed.
p. cm.
Summary: While a serial killer stalks his small Georgia town, sixteen-year-old Henry tries to find the truth about the terrible accident that robbed him of his mother and his memories, aided by his friend Justine but not by his distant father.
ISBN 978-0-7387-3336-4
[1. Amnesia—Fiction. 2. Fathers and sons—Fiction. 3. Identity—Fiction. 4. Serial murderers—Fiction. 5. Medical care—Fiction. 6. Family life—Georgia—Fiction. 7. Georgia—Fiction.] I. Title.
PZ7.S15415Hen 2012
[Fic]—dc23

2012009865

Flux
Llewellyn Worldwide Ltd.
2143 Wooddale Drive
Woodbury, MN 55125-2989
www.fluxnow.com

Printed in the United States of America

To my wife, Anna Michelle Salomon, and our three sons:
Andre Logan, Joshua Kyle, and Adin Jeremy.

one

XXX

Spanish moss, bleached to gray in the heat, stretched down from the trees and the breeze barely stirred the air. From his bedroom window, Henry watched oak branches reaching for the house, close enough to scratch against the bricks. The marshes surrounding St. Simons Island stretched to the horizon, flashing with light where the rising sun reflected off the water.

With the blinds pulled up, he pressed his hands against the glass. Scar tissue ringed his index finger like jewelry made of flesh, matching the bracelet on his left wrist and the necklace of scars circling his neck. More snaked around his legs, beading with sweat in the Georgia heat.

Henry closed his eyes, took a deep breath, and then

counted to ten. A pushpin stuck out of the wall next to the window and he grabbed it without looking. A branch grated across the house with a hiss that seemed almost alive.

Where the sharp metal point broke the skin of his right index finger, a single bead of blood welled up. He opened his eyes, took another breath, and then counted again.

Pressing against the glass, he pushed the pin the rest of the way into his finger. Blood ran like rain down the window, but Henry Franks didn't feel a thing.

He stumbled through the doorway to Brunswick High School as everyone rushed inside to get out of the heat. "Watch where you're going," someone said without turning around. Henry's backpack slid off his shoulders and, thankfully, stayed zipped when someone else kicked it out of the way. On his knees, he clutched the pack to his chest as classmates walked around him.

"Breathe, Henry," he said as a slim hand appeared before his half-open eyes. Pink nails and long fingers reached toward him. When he looked up, his next-door neighbor's smile was as warm as always. Her shoulder-length brown hair was tied up for summer, exposing far too much skin, and he couldn't figure out where to rest his eyes.

"Come here often?" Justine asked, letting her hand fall back to her side as he stood up on his own.

Henry shrugged. "It's the law," he said, staring at the

floor. Her toenails were painted pink as well, and when he finally looked up at her, she was smiling. "You match."

She laughed as the homeroom bell rang and then waved before running down the hall to her class.

"Breathe," he said again, as she turned the corner and disappeared from view.

Snow and ice flashed across the screen but, as Henry looked around the science lab, it was obvious no one was paying attention to the movie. A gap in the miniblinds gave a view of the picnic area where lunch was already being served, a haze of heat floating off the cement. In the back of the room, students had their feet on the tables and their eyes closed. At her desk, the teacher read over some paperwork, red pen in hand.

Second row, third seat over, Henry kept his head down, watching his classmates through unruly brown hair that kept falling into his eyes. In the heat, his scars itched, and he clenched his fingers into a fist to keep from scratching.

Four thousand, three hundred and seventeen stitches, his father had told him once. All the King's horses and all the King's men had put Henry Franks back together again.

Next to him, a cheerleader scribbled in her notebook while chewing on a long blond ponytail. As he tried not to watch, she ripped the paper out, one inch at a time to keep down the noise, then folded it up. She looked at the teacher, stretched her hand out, and dropped the note on Henry's desk.

The small square sat there, resting on the desk's edge, and he stared at it, unaware he was holding his breath. His fingers, busy rubbing the scar circling his wrist, ceased their movement before crawling across to the note.

In the darkness, he had to squint to make out the writing on the outside, but his eyes weren't all that great to begin with. Still, as he unfolded it, he felt the lines where her pen had pressed too hard against the paper.

He could sense her watching him, as though she was trying to tell him something but didn't want to make a sound during the movie, and the sensation was a warm heat against his skin.

Inside, the words were easier to read, but she slid down in her chair and kicked him under his desk before he even started. When Henry looked over, she made shooing motions with her hands and pointed to the other side of him.

He turned around. Bobby Dixon, at the next desk over and wearing his football jersey as usual, had his hand out, waiting for the note. Head down, Henry refolded the paper and passed it over, unable to look at either of them.

From behind him, he felt a tap on his shoulder before another student slid a ripped piece of paper down his arm. Even in the dim light, the words were easy to read:

Did you really think her note was for you?

On the bus ride home, he sat alone as always and thought about invisibility until Justine took the seat in front of him.

"I heard." She turned to face him, her arms on the back of the bench. "Small school."

Henry looked out the window and shrugged. "Been that kind of life."

"Could've been worse," she said, then turned away from him as the bus started moving.

"How?" he asked, but the question was drowned out by the diesel engine. He pushed himself up and leaned forward to talk to her.

"How?" he repeated.

She looked back at him and smiled, lighting up her soft brown eyes. "Could've been a longer movie."

She was a sophomore, too, but not in any of his classes, and she was the one person at school who seemed to know his name, mostly because she lived in the house next door to him. She knew everyone, it seemed, and he was … well, he was Henry.

"Any plans for summer?" she asked.

Henry opened his mouth, though he didn't have an answer. No plans, ever.

"Football practice," came from the seat behind him. Bobby stretched his arms over Henry, pushing him out of the way in order to drum a quick beat on Justine's backpack where it sat beside her. "You cheering again?"

Henry squeezed up against the window as they drove over the only bridge onto St. Simons and Bobby's elbow kept hitting his shoulder. In the heat of the bus, his shirt was sticking to his skin and the thin white scar that circled his neck appeared for a moment when he pulled the collar out, but he quickly hid it away.

Justine pushed her backpack to the floor, breaking the beat. "No, my parents didn't appreciate the three Bs I got this year. They decided I would get better grades without distractions."

The bus stopped with a squeal of hydraulics and Henry ducked beneath Bobby's arm.

"Bye," Bobby said, slapping Henry's shoulder and pushing him forward so that he stumbled down the aisle. Someone laughed, but he didn't turn around to see who it was.

"Henry," Justine called to him as he walked down the street.

He stopped walking but, for a long moment, didn't turn around. When he looked over his shoulder at her, she was lost in the shadows of the oak trees lining the street.

"Are you all right?" she asked.

Henry shook his head before turning around to face her.

"I was actually asking you," she said, taking a step closer to him, "on the bus, about summer."

He let his hair fall into his eyes before finally brushing it away. "No plans," he said. "You?"

"Junior counselor at the Y camp, that's about it." She walked a little in front of him, maintaining most of the conversation as usual. "I overheard my parents talking about a trip somewhere but I didn't pay much attention."

He turned into his yard even as she was speaking, and

as he walked up to his house he could still hear her as she continued walking home.

Henry waved, even though she had already disappeared inside, and slipped his key into the lock. He jiggled the handle up and to the right, then turned the knob. Repeat steps two and three as needed. A bare bulb burned right inside the door, the weak light reflecting off the dark wood paneling and darker floor with a strange yellow tinge. Curtains, thick and dusty, were pulled across the windows and allowed knives of sunlight to sneak through and slant across the room. Dust danced and tumbled around him as he walked down the hall. Spanish moss fell against the windows, adding a diseased pallor to the heavy air.

Upstairs, Henry closed his bedroom door, dropped his backpack on the bed, and slid down to the floor. The room was sparsely furnished: a small desk with a laptop attached to an LCD monitor, and mismatched furniture. There had been a mirror over his dresser once but he'd taken it down, leaving blank walls dotted with pushpins around his desk.

He'd put the mirror in the closet after studying his body for hours one night, trying to see all of the scars or count the stitches or remember the accident.

He'd failed at all three and vowed never to try again.

From a pile next to him, he pulled out a scrapbook and flipped to the back; to a picture of him surrounded by boys and girls he didn't recognize at a birthday party he had no memory of ever attending. He was blowing out the candles and they were all smiling when the flash caught the moment. They were, he thought, friends.

Outside, a branch scraped against the house. Henry gently pushed the scrapbook away, unwilling to further damage the book after so many nights flipping the pages. He walked to the window and scrubbed the dried blood off the glass, then rested his finger on a plastic pushpin. He took a deep breath and counted to ten. The hissing grew louder but there was no wind and the trees were still.

Margaret Saville, PhD
St. Simons Island, Glynn County, GA
Tuesday, May 5, 2009
Patient: Henry Franks
(DOB: November 19, 1992)

Official record of nine-month therapeutic anniversary: patient presents with retrograde amnesia affecting declarative memory. Medical consultation shows no physical damage to medial temporal lobe or hippocampus; diagnosis of post-traumatic stress from motor vehicle accident (patient spent extended period of time comatose after accident, mother did not survive).

Continued monitoring of occasional blackout phenomenon in addition to twice-weekly therapy to accept the possibility of permanent memory loss.

With his index finger, the skin a shade or two darker than the rest of his hand, Henry scratched at the heavy line crossing his left wrist.

"They itch?" Dr. Saville asked.

"Always," he said before curling his mismatched fingers into a fist to stop the motion. Sweat beaded on his skin, pooling in the scars.

"Why can't I remember?" he asked.

"It's a process, Henry, the act of remembering.

The accident, and before—the memories are there. It's only been a year." She pointed to the photograph he'd brought, resting on the table between them: Henry and his parents, bright smiles and wind-blown hair. "Have you had the dream again?"

"No." Henry closed his eyes. His discolored finger came to rest on the scar around his neck and he lowered his head to try to hide the movement and the thin white line. "A new one."

"Want to talk about it?"

"No." He opened his eyes and looked out the window, anywhere but at the doctor. The heat lay heavy on the drooping palm fronds outside the window, a haze shimmering off a white pathway through the trees.

"Henry," she said.

He took a deep breath, silently counting to ten. "There's a girl."

"Someone from school?"

"No," he said, his voice rougher than he'd intended. "No. She's a child, with pigtails."

"Do you recognize her?"

He leaned forward; heavy bangs in need of a haircut fell in front of his eyes. Safe behind their barrier, he said, "I can't remember." His fingers clutched at the fabric of the couch as he rested his head back into the cushion.

"Deep breaths, Henry, it's all right. Count to ten, like we've been practicing."

Eyes closed, his lips moved as he collapsed in on himself, tucking his face between his drawn-up knees.

"She called me Daddy. Why can't I remember her name?" he asked.

"It was just a dream."

"She felt so alive; real, so much more than just a dream."

From the desk, the alarm on the clock beeped once, loud in the office. Henry jumped at the sound, and then brushed the hair out of his face.

"Time?"

Dr. Saville nodded. "That all right?"

He shrugged, then stood up, fingers tight on the photograph.

"I talked to your dad, Henry" she said, "about Thursday. We'll have to meet Friday this week."

He nodded without looking at her.

"Next week we'll go back to Tuesday, Thursday. Don't forget your breathing exercises when you start to panic. They're important."

"I know," he said. "It's everything else I forget."

two

XXX

His father was sitting at the table when Henry went downstairs for dinner. Two places were set, thick plastic dishes warped, cracked, and better than anything else they owned. Fast food burgers sat, unwrapped, on the plates, with packets of ketchup, mustard, and relish piled in the middle of the table.

Around a mouthful of food, his father smiled. "Dinnertime."

Henry sat down, dressed his burger and began to eat, keeping an eye on his father as they sat across from each other.

"Have you been taking your meds?" His father's white consultation jacket had seen better days. A faded Southeast

Georgia Regional Medical Center patch was coming loose, just a little right of center.

"Yes."

When his father smiled again, Henry looked down at his empty plate before reaching for another burger.

"Appetite's back?"

Henry shrugged. "It helps."

"Some of the medications have stomach side effects."

"Eating helps," Henry said.

"And the itching?"

"Scratching helps too."

"Need more ointment?"

Henry shook his head, dark hair falling into his face and he left it there.

"Stronger?" his father asked. "I can make it stronger next time, if you'd like. Or not, whatever you need."

Henry shrugged again and then pushed the plate of food away without taking anything.

"You can eat it if you want."

"I'm not hungry."

"Would you be if I wasn't here?" His father's hands rested on the table, playing with the plastic silverware, the skin white where he gripped the knife and fork too tightly.

Henry shook his head and reached for the food.

"Henry?"

"Sorry," he said, around the first bite of the second burger.

"Me too," his father said.

He stopped chewing long enough to look up at his father.

"Really, Henry, I'm sorry. Has Dr. Saville helped?"

With the rest of the burger in his hand, Henry stood. The metal chair folded in on itself and clattered to the floor. His father rushed around to pick it up.

"It's okay," Henry said, but his father unfolded the chair and slid it back into place anyway.

"My fault," his father said.

"Stop saying that."

"What?" His father looked at him, a frown drawing ever-deeper lines into his skin.

"That you're sorry."

"What would you like me to say, Henry?"

"Anything but that."

"Dr. Saville?"

"I still don't remember," he said, turning to walk out the door. "But I'm fine with that now."

Henry sat in his room, staring at a blank monitor, fingers resting on the keyboard. A branch beat against the window in the summer wind, the sound harsh and grating. He spun around in his chair, knocking a plastic pillbox to the ground. In the small room, it only took a couple of steps for him to reach the window and pull up the blinds. A sliver of moon surrounded by haze glowed above the tree line.

Across the backyard, through the branches, he could

see a part of Justine's house but the lights were off. He raised the window, and the noise of the leaves grew louder as branches skittered against the house. In the heat, he scratched at the scar around his neck.

Leaving the window, he moved the mouse to wake his computer up but focused on nothing beyond the lingering images of the dream. A ghost of a memory, a little girl calling him Daddy. And then, like his life, she was gone.

He took a deep breath. Another, counting to ten as he struggled to hold on to the memories until all that remained was his father's voice, telling him about a life he couldn't remember and a death he'd somehow forgotten.

three

XXX

William Franks rested his head in his hands, staring at his half-eaten dinner without seeing it. He rubbed his fingers into the skin of his temples, trying to knead the headache away. It didn't help. He turned to look at the empty doorway that Henry had just walked through, trying to see even a shadow of his son, but there was nothing there.

"I'm sorry," he said, the words quiet in the stillness of the empty room.

The headache never seemed to go away lately. He sighed as he turned the lights off, blinking in a short moment of relief from the brightness before heading to the kitchen. He pushed the toaster to the side and pulled out another bag of fast food. From the cabinet above the fridge ketchup and spread some on two them back up.

he back door, pushing the curtain out into the yard. Shadows blan- was difficult to see. He rested his :h but didn't turn it on.

:ound him, with soft squeaks from upstairs and the steady hum of the :ed out the window until his eyes ly then did he turn the light on, and banishing the gloom. With a deep breath, he unlocked the door, opening it slowly to cut down on the noise from the hinges.

The heat hit almost immediately, moist and almost too thick to breathe, hurting his lungs with each inhale. The pounding in his head returned with a vengeance, every beat of his heart stabbing through him. William took one step outside and placed the fast food bag on the back stoop, never taking his eyes off the shadows hiding behind the trees. His pulse raced as he slammed the door shut behind him.

He took deep gasping breaths as his fingers crawled up the wall toward the light switch, flicking it down and plunging the yard back into darkness. Only then did he turn around and look out the window. Nothing moved beyond the swaying of the branches, brushing against the side of the house in the breeze.

Half an hour later he was still standing there, and the bag of food sat on the stoop untouched. William sighed. He rubbed his palms into his eyes until he saw stars but it didn't help the pounding. Grabbing his keys, he walked out the front door, closing it as softly as he could. In his car, he rested his head back against the seat, staring at nothing before finally backing out of the driveway.

He drove slowly through Harrison Pointe, his neck on a swivel trying to see between every house, searching the shadows. William forced himself not to blink, unwilling to risk missing something. From the glove box he took out a flashlight and held it out the open window, shining the light around so he could see better. It didn't help.

Up and down Frederica, the flashlight beam moving in circles. Turning onto Sea Island Road, he studied the marshes until he reached Torras Causeway and continued his search on the mainland. He turned onto K Street and parked, closing his eyes long enough to lessen the pounding. Even with the air on high, it was too hot in the car. Still, he managed to doze off, waking with a start as the first hint of the sun broke over the horizon.

Turning from K Street onto Putnam, he slammed on the brakes as a lone figure staggered out of the trees at the end of the road. Long hair flew out behind it in the wind. William jumped out of the car, running to catch up as the person walked into a house.

Sheriff Calls Brunswick Murder Scene "Appalling"

BRUNSWICK, GA—June 3, 2009: The mysterious death of a Brunswick woman has now become a murder investigation. Sylvia Foote, 41, was found beaten to death at her home Sunday morning. Forensic teams were still searching her house Tuesday for evidence, and Assistant District Attorney of Glynn County Brian Winters said that investigators plan to return to the Brunswick home on Wednesday as they try to figure out how and why Foote was killed.

"From our perspective, this is being treated with the highest priority," Winters said.

An autopsy revealed that Foote died of multiple wounds and blunt force trauma. "The state forensics crime lab has been called in and they will be up at the scene doing some specialized searches," Glynn County Sheriff Dan Bailey said, calling the scene one of the worst he'd ever had to investigate.

The death of the popular teacher and mother of three has hit the community hard, as people continue to leave flowers and candles outside her home and at Brunswick High School, where she taught science and was instrumental in developing the Jekyll Island Sea Turtle Tracking curriculum for the district.

Winters said that they have interviewed dozens of people. "It's a process that takes some time." He also announced a $5,000 reward for information leading to an arrest in the case.

2009 Hurricane Season Predicted to be Active (Update)

MIAMI, FL—June 3, 2009: The National Hurricane Center has released their updated hurricane predictions as the 2009 Hurricane Season began June 1. Original forecasts called for 12–18 named storms with 3–5 having the potential to strike the United States. The update has increased the number of total named storms to 14–20 while lowering the risk to the United States to 2–4.

Margaret Saville, PhD
St. Simons Island, Glynn County, GA
Thursday, June 4, 2009
Patient: Henry Franks
(DOB: November 19, 1992)

A palm frond brushed against the glass, stirred by the thin summer wind that had dropped the temperature into the high eighties. Henry flinched at the sound, his fingers rigid where they pressed against his legs.

"Breathe, Henry," he said, hunched over so far he was talking to his shoes.

"Relax," Dr. Saville said. "You're safe here."

He looked up at her, his pale gray eyes red from too many sleepless nights. His skin was dusky olive above the thin white scar on his neck and pale white below it, where the V of his shirt showed part of his chest.

He took a breath, counted to ten, exhaled.

"Any vacation plans now that school is out?" Dr. Saville reached for her pen and loudly clicked it open, waiting.

"No." As he shook his head, brown hair swirled away from his face and he smiled. "I know, Doctor," he said, "no one-word answers. I remember that."

She smiled in reply and the pen flew across the paper. "So, what about Justine?"

"She's a friend, I guess."

"Friends are good."

"Girlfriends are better," he said, and let his hair fall back into his eyes.

"Anyone in particular?"

"No, no one. Not yet."

"Does 'no one' have a name?"

Henry scratched his wrist with his discolored finger, then clenched his hands together. "No."

"Want to talk about it?"

"I don't think anyone at school even knows my name," Henry said before brushing the hair back from his eyes.

"Justine does."

"She lives next door, she has to." He smiled as the sun broke through the clouds and lightened the room. The palm frond brushing against the window fell silent.

"She has to be friends with you?"

"No, I guess not."

"Does she talk to you?" Dr. Saville asked.

He laughed. "It's Justine. All she does is talk."

"That's good, right?"

"Good?"

"Her talking to you, Henry," she said. "How would you feel if she stopped?"

He took a deep breath, and then rubbed his hands over his face. "Doesn't help."

"With?"

"Life? Memory?"

"Dreams?"

He slid down in his seat, hiding behind his hair as he tensed up. He nodded, once.

"The old dream, Henry?"

Again, the nod.

"How long has it been? Months?" She flipped through her notebook, then tapped her pen against her leg. "Did something happen?"

Henry looked at her, and then reached for his backpack. He pulled out a card and handed it to her.

HAPPY FIRST BIRTHDAY, SON! blared a smiling cartoon father balancing a cake on a unicycle.

Dr. Saville read the card, then passed it back.

"He gave it to me yesterday," Henry said.

"Why?"

"I woke up a year ago."

"Then the dream last night?" she asked.

"Again."

"Anything new?"

"I didn't die," Henry said. "Does that count?"

"Well, that's something, at least," Dr. Saville said. "Anything else?"

"She died this time."

four

XXX

From where Henry lay on his bed, he watched the sunlight cast shadows on the wall. It was already hot, despite central air and the ceiling fan, and even in boxers and a T-shirt, he'd woken up drenched in sweat. Scars like railroad tracks leading nowhere circled around his legs and itched in the heat.

Out his window he had a view of a corner of Justine's front yard where her younger brother was bouncing a ball against their house. Justine was nowhere to be seen. He closed the blinds, dry-swallowed his pills, and walked downstairs in the empty house. A bowl sat on the table next to a box of cereal, waiting for him, but his father had long since left for work. A piece of paper fluttered to the ground when he pulled his chair out.

Henry, he read as he poured the milk, *Sorry about the card.*

From the street, a car blew its horn, and Henry walked to the front door to look outside. A pickup truck, overloaded with cheerleaders, sat in front of Justine's house. As he watched, she jumped into the back and then they were gone. Her brother continued bouncing his ball as Henry went back to breakfast.

He pulled the card out of his backpack and leaned it against the base of his monitor. One year. He rested the tip of his finger on one of the pushpins, staring at the patchwork flesh of his hand. The more he stared at it, the stranger it looked. The scar interrupted the lines on his palm, no longer telling any future he could imagine. Only the past interested him anymore. His own past. Even his name seemed to weigh strangely on him and the more he repeated it to himself, the less it seemed like a real word at all.

The scrapbook lay where he'd left it, open to the picture of his mother, but no matter how long he studied her face, he couldn't remember her; it was as if a stranger held his hand. Even his own face was alien to him, and he'd spent hours one night looking at his reflection trying to remember himself. He'd cried himself to sleep that night, face buried in the pillow, afraid his father would hear his sobs.

Beneath the picture, his father had written *Mommy, Daddy, Henry* with a ballpoint pen. The pages were falling out of the book due to how often he flipped through it; the flimsy photo album was in danger of falling apart completely. Henry ran his finger over the words but couldn't feel a thing, and suddenly realized he didn't even know his mother's name.

He took the stairs two at a time, jumping down them and calling for his father. "Dad!" echoed through the empty house. Where the hallway to the master bedroom began, Henry stopped. A wooden door stood at the end of the short hallway, a deadbolt lock above the knob. Henry took a deep breath, stepped forward, and knocked.

The house was silent save for the constant hum of the air-conditioner.

His hand rested on the doorknob; he closed his eyes as he tried to open it and failed.

Hours later, when he heard his father return home, Henry started downstairs. The question of his mother's name was on the tip of his tongue but would remain unasked. When his father's voice drifted up the stairs, Henry stopped in the shadows halfway down, trying to see the person his father was talking to.

"C6, C7," his father said while emptying three bags

of fast food out on the table. "Carbamazepine and phenobarbitol; maybe divalproex. C6, C7. So close, sweetheart, almost there, I promise." But as far as Henry could see, there was no one else in the room.

Dr. Franks piled the hamburgers up on the counter, then filled one bag back up and started walking to the dining room with it, grabbing a handful of ketchup packets on the way.

Henry watched, barely able to breathe, as his father placed the burgers on the table.

"Dinner," his father said, calling up to him.

He tiptoed back up to his room and then walked downstairs. By the time he reached the kitchen, the remaining pile of burgers on the counter was gone. On the dining room table there were only enough for their dinner. His father was already eating.

As Henry looked at him, for just a moment, he thought he was staring at a stranger.

After dinner, his father cleaned the table and then left the room. The deadbolt clicking into place on his father's door was loud in the silence. Henry sat at the empty table, the question of his mother's name still unspoken and barely more than a memory.

Wind brushed leaves against the windows in the humid summer evening as the sun dipped beneath the horizon. In the kitchen, Henry searched for the rest of the food his father had brought home, but there was only one bag in the garbage can and no evidence remained that there had been any other hamburgers in the house.

Somewhere, a dog barked. Then, with a crash of a branch against the side of the house, the wind hissed right outside the window.

Henry pushed the mini-blinds to the side and peered out into the backyard. A light from Justine's house sent hazy shadows across the summer-scorched grass. Barely visible from where he was standing, there was a bag of fast food on the back stoop.

Henry dropped the blinds, staring at nothing while the image of that bag flashed across his vision every time he blinked. He took a deep breath before walking to the back door and flipping the light switch for the backyard.

The single halogen flooded the area with light. A weak breeze stirred as Henry opened the door. He picked the fast food bag up. Aside from crumpled wrappers, it was empty. He dropped it to the ground and took another look around the yard.

Old oak trees, gnarled roots poking out of the ground, were draped with Spanish moss. An ancient iron fence, more rusted than not, in some places ran right into the trees in its circuit of the yard. A gate swung open on broken hinges. Even at night, the heat brought beads of sweat out on his skin, catching in the scars.

A branch snapped in two as it clawed against the house and he hurried inside, locking the door behind him. He took another deep breath, counting to ten as he leaned against the wall, staring out between the miniblinds as the Spanish moss hung motionless in the still night air.

Margaret Saville, PhD
St. Simons Island, Glynn County, GA
Tuesday, August 4, 2009
Patient: Henry Franks
(DOB: November 19, 1992)

"I'm alive," he said. "I breathe."

"And the dream?" Dr. Saville asked.

"I'm living the wrong life." He sat up, hair falling into his face, and he tensed his fingers, stretching them as far as they would go. Then, with a shrug, he slumped back down, melting into the cushion. "Or something like that. It's me but it's not me. Then I wake up."

"This is part of the process, Henry."

"Waking up is good."

"Then what?"

He looked at her, then closed his eyes. "Nothing. No dreams during the day. You need memories for that, don't you?"

"What do you do during the day?"

"I'm not exactly the beach type," he said. "Sat out back last week where no one could see. Only part of me tanned."

"Hang out with friends? Justine?"

He looked toward the window, where the palm tree brushed along the glass, and then shrugged. "She always says hi, I guess."

"Do you talk to her when she talks to you?" Dr. Saville asked.

"She has her own friends." He shook his head. "I have ... "

"You have?" she asked, when he didn't continue.

"Was going to say my father, but he's usually MIA, so it's just me."

"Do you think you have any friends?"

"I have pictures of friends in the scrapbook he put together. And nightmares. But I don't recognize anyone from the photographs."

"Has anyone from the album appeared in a dream?" she asked.

He stared back out the window past the palms to the sliver of the Atlantic visible between the other buildings. The distant horizon shimmered in the haze.

"Mom."

"She's the only person you recognize?"

"No." He shook his head, once more hiding behind his hair.

"Who?"

"The little girl. Calling me Daddy, over and over again."

"She's in your scrapbook?" Dr. Saville asked.

"No, but I always think I know her."

"Do you?"

He shrugged. "Her name's Elizabeth."

"Elizabeth?"

"She told me."

"You asked?"

He smiled. "Why not, it's my dream." Then the smile died. "I think."

"You think?"

"I asked her what my name was."

"And?"

"She called me Daddy again."

"That's progress."

"I asked her what Mommy called me."

Dr. Saville's pen stopped its steady march across the paper and she looked up at him. Her brown hair, lighter in the summer months, was plastered to her scalp and didn't move with the motion. "'Mommy'?"

"She started to cry."

"Did you wake up?" Dr. Saville asked.

"'Victor,' Elizabeth said. 'Mommy called you Victor before she died.'"

Henry pushed himself up so hard that the heavy couch actually moved across the wooden floor. He walked to the window, watching the heat radiating in waves off the white stone pathway beyond the palm tree. The path wandered into the bushes and stopped. It was, he thought, symbolic of something; this meaningless walkway behind a psychologist's office, boldly going nowhere. Like his life.

"Ready for school?" Dr. Saville asked after too long a silence.

He didn't look at her. "It's school."

"New year, new opportunities."

"Joy," he said, hiding his smile from her.

"Your father asked me to speak to you about the future, Henry. You're a junior now, only two years until college."

"I know."

"And?"

"And?" he asked.

"The future?"

"I have enough problems with the past." Then he laughed, the sound thin and weak.

"Henry," she said.

"Maybe in the future, I have a daughter." He looked at her. "I think I'll call her Elizabeth."

"That's not quite what your father meant, but we can talk about that if you'd like."

"Is this my last session?"

"Do you want it to be?" she asked. "My understanding is you'll continue to come after school, the way you did last year."

Henry looked back out the window. "Will it help?"

"I'd like to think so."

Henry walked back to the couch and sat down, pressing his palms into his thighs. Closed his eyes and counted to ten.

"Did Elizabeth say anything else?" Dr. Saville asked.

He opened his eyes, looking at her through the fall of his hair. "I had to protect her," he said, his voice harsh. "She's my daughter."

"You're not Victor," Dr. Saville said, her pen still and silent above the paper.

"I had to." He rested his head back, exposing his neck. He swallowed and the scar writhed. "I couldn't let her die like that."

"Tell me what happened, Henry."

"I killed her."

"Who?" she said, the single word barely spoken out loud.

"I killed them all."

"Henry?"

"Then I woke up." He smiled. "I killed my mother."

"What happened to Elizabeth?"

"I held her while she died."

Discovery of Bodies Closes Popular Beach

Jekyll Island, GA—August 6, 2009: The bodies of two missing boaters washed ashore on Jekyll Island early Wednesday morning. Missing since late Monday night, they were discovered caught in the driftwood by Darius Martin, a local fisherman.

Nancy Woods, of the Jekyll Island Parks Services, said that preliminary information was still being gathered but that their boat, which has yet to be located, might answer further questions.

The two boaters, Crayton Mission, 52, and his nephew Paul Wislon, 24, were reported missing late Saturday night by Wanda Mission, wife of Crayton.

As of this time, foul play is not suspected.

Five

XXX

The piece of paper hidden beneath his pillbox had two words on it: *Victor, Elizabeth.* Out of curiosity, he'd Googled the names, but there were too many hits to realistically count. Henry dry-swallowed his medications, took a single look at the names, then folded the paper back up before sliding it into place beneath the plastic box.

"Victor," he said. The word seemed weightless, without meaning. A stranger's name. It felt wrong when said out loud, unreal.

His father had left for work by the time he ventured downstairs, and he rushed through breakfast even though he had nothing else to do all day long other than sweat and eat.

He stood on the front porch, watching Justine's brother jumping through a sprinkler, and briefly considered mowing the lawn just to see if his father would notice.

"You can join us." Her voice came from behind him and he gripped the rusted metal railing to keep from jumping out his skin. "Not dressed like that, of course, but you're welcome to jump in. The water's, well, not hot, at least."

Justine walked up to the side of the porch and when he turned his head, she was closer than he'd expected her to be. Her hair was tied up and the sun glinted off the tiny gold hoops in her ears and for a moment he forgot to breathe.

"You do know it's summer, right?" she asked. "You know, heat, humidity. Did I mention heat?"

Henry brushed the hair out of his eyes and tried, but failed, not to stare. Cut-offs left long tan legs glowing in the morning sun. A pink bikini top was visible through her white T-shirt. Honey-brown eyes and a welcoming smile. He couldn't figure out where to look, so he let the hair fall back down.

"I'm familiar with the concept," he said with a shrug. "I'm not really a summer person."

"You're in blue jeans and a T-shirt," she said. "In August. As far as I can tell, you're a mammal."

He laughed. "I'm usually inside, where it's air-conditioned."

Justine looked around, taking in the entire porch. "I

know, you're part hermit. But you do realize that you're actually outside at the moment?"

He mimicked her motions of looking around. "My dad took me to Jekyll last week. That was outside."

"Did you actually go on the beach?"

"Drove past it. Does that count?"

She smiled. "No." Sunlight glistened on pink lips and white teeth and golden skin.

He breathed, counted to ten in silence, and tried to return her smile.

"Want to join us in the sprinkler?" she asked again, turning to walk back to her yard. With one motion, she took her T-shirt off and dropped it to the ground. "Coming, Henry?" she said over her shoulder.

He went down the steps two at a time, and then stopped on the sidewalk, watching Justine jump through the sprinkler in her wet denim cut-offs and pink bikini top. He picked up her T-shirt as he walked into the water, holding it in his hand as he let the water rain down on him, soaking his jeans. His hair plastered itself to his face, hanging down his neck, and he brushed it back and looked up at the sun, burning down on his pale skin.

He smiled.

"If I wanted my shirt wet, I'd have left it on," she said, pulling it out of his grasp.

Henry looked at it and shrugged. "You dropped it."

She laughed. "Not that I'm complaining. You've been inside all summer and I finally got you in the sprinkler. My vacation is a success."

"You always could have knocked," he said.

Justine threw her wet shirt at him. "I don't knock."

The shirt landed on his face and, for a moment, all he saw was white. So faintly it might have been his imagination, he could smell her on the fabric.

"Why not?" he asked, through her shirt, before taking it off.

"Well, one, my mom might kill me. Or at least ground me for what little remains of vacation if I did anything, anything at all, that she would consider to be even remotely improper." She smiled, holding her hand out for her shirt. "Two, I obviously didn't have to; you're here."

"Improper?" Henry held her shirt up, looking at her wet hair hanging on her bare shoulders.

"Well, her definition and mine aren't quite the same thing."

He threw the shirt back, jumped through the sprinkler one more time, and then started walking back to his house.

"Henry?" she called out to him.

When he turned around, she was sliding back into her T-shirt. It clung to her skin and he could still see the pink bikini top through the wet fabric.

"Just because I don't knock doesn't mean you can't," she said, before smiling one more time and then running inside her house.

six

XXX

His shirt glued itself to his skin within moments of leaving the house, and he was sure his deodorant had failed before the school bus even arrived. After standing on the sidewalk too long, the bottoms of his sneakers seemed to adhere to the concrete and the first step onto the bus was sticky.

Justine melted into the seat in front him. She fought with the window and gave up with it open almost an entire inch. The August breeze through the opening was hot against his face. Her brown hair was up, as always, exposing a great deal of tan neck all the way down to the straps of her tank top. One thin river of sweat began with a single bead at the base of her hair and disappeared down her back.

She fanned herself with her hand and then turned around to face him. “Think of ice,” she said. “Milk shakes, chocolate ice cream, snow. Have you ever seen snow?”

“No.” Henry shook his head.

“Really? We go up north to see family for Thanksgiving and it snows sometimes. Whose bright idea was it, do you think, to put plastic seats on a bus in Georgia? I’m sticking to the seat, here. Is that why you’re in jeans again?”

Henry shrugged and Justine, as usual, continued her monologue.

“I’m pretty sure I’ll be in shorts through November at least. Then we’ll get a few weeks of fall, a week or two of winter, and then it’s summer again. So you’ve never seen snow?”

He shook his head.

“You weren’t on the bus yesterday afternoon.”

“It was Thursday.”

“I know. Tuesday, Thursday, Henry’s not on the bus home; same as last year. Why not?”

She rode half-turned in her seat, one arm curled around the backrest, the plastic piping on the vinyl biting into her skin. Her white bra strap slipped out from the white shirt. He couldn’t meet her eyes and kept looking at the strap.

“Doctor,” he said to her shoulder. His wrist itched as the medicinal mint smell of the ointment lingered on his fingers and around his neck.

“For your scars?” she asked. “I thought I should ask, but then, no, I figured, if you wanted to talk about it, you would. Of course, I told myself, 'Justine, he doesn't actually talk all that much. You should probably ask.'"

He tilted his head to the side, the way a dog looks at a human when spoken to, then covered his mouth to try not to laugh. It didn't work.

"It's a curse, my mom says." Justine smiled. "There's even a term for it."

"There is?" he asked.

"It's called a sense of humor."

Henry shook his head and laughed, then went back to studying the way her white bra strap seemed to glow against her tan skin.

"So," she said, "the scars?"

"I don't remember," he said, the words barely spoken out loud.

"What?"

"The accident."

"Accident?" she asked, reaching her arm out, but she let it fall short without touching him.

He shrugged and turned to look out the window. "So they tell me."

"I have a scar too," she said as they pulled into the parking lot, pointing at her stomach, hidden by her tank top. "Appendix, when I was five. I don't really remember it."

"Might be better not to remember," he said.

He looked at where her fingers lingered on her own wrist, right about where his own scars were. When he glanced back up, she was watching him.

"They're only scars, Henry," she said. "They don't change who you are."

With a shriek of brakes, the bus shuddered to a stop. One of her friends called her name and she jumped up and ran off the bus. Henry waited until almost everyone had left before standing up. It was sweat, he thought, not tears he was wiping from his eyes.

Just sweat.

Murder on Jekyll Island Has Not Impacted Tourist Season

Jekyll Island, GA—August 14, 2009: Preliminary autopsy reports on the two boaters, Crayton Mission, 52, and his nephew Paul Wislon, 24, found on Jekyll Island on August 5 have, according to Brunswick Police Department spokesperson Carmella Rawls, ruled out drowning as the cause of death.

"We have opened up an investigation into the murder of Mr. Mission and Mr. Wislon," Rawls stated in an impromptu press conference.

Assistant District Attorney Brian Winters gave a brusque "No comment" when asked if there were any leads.

FLETC, the Federal Law Enforcement Training Center, located in Brunswick, has provided logistical and material support to the investigation in order to locate the boat that Mission and Wislon were supposed to be on.

Wanda Mission and her brother, Jerome Craw, were questioned for background but neither is considered a suspect in the deaths at this time, according to sources close to the investigation.

seven

Justine bounced into the seat in front of him, the plastic bench squeaking in protest at the early morning activity. Her tank top, pink today, slipped down as always, exposing a matching pink bra strap.

Henry glanced up, but only for a moment before returning his gaze to her shoulder, unable, unwilling, to meet her warm honey eyes.

"Seriously, did you think to yourself, 'Henry, it's hotter than hell out there; today's menu choices are black with varying shades of black in some sort of gothic monochromatic thing or well, damn, black it is.'"

She smiled; little white teeth, the very tip of a small pink tongue were surrounded by lips colored just a shade different from her shirt. His gaze returned to her shoulder, maybe her neck, anywhere but to those welcoming eyes and too-long lashes and that smile.

"Gothic?" he asked.

"That's not the look you're going for?"

"I've got a look?"

She smiled again. Most amazing of all, he smiled back. In his lap, his off-colored finger scratched along the scar on his left wrist; mint and shame wiped the smile off his face.

The bus pulled to a stop on Gloucester to pick up more students, and Justine turned to the window.

"Henry?" she asked, pointing toward one of the small tables in front of the sidewalk cafes. "Isn't that your dad?"

The bus started pulling away and Henry pressed up to the glass for a better view, but all he saw was the woman the man was sitting with. He blinked and the bus turned the corner. *Dr. Saville?*

"Kind of looked like him, but..." Justine shrugged.

Henry stared out the window, trying to count to ten, the numbers running together until he lost count. He took a deep breath. Another. His fingers ran over his scars and Justine reached her hand out almost far enough to touch his arm.

"Do they hurt?"

He froze, then raised his hand to rest upon the scar around his neck. He pulled his collar up to cover the line. Still, she smiled at him. He tried, but failed, to smile back.

"They itch," he said. "Sometimes."

"I'm sorry."

"'He jests at scars that never felt a wound.'"

"Wait, I know that," she said, her hand in his face to keep him from speaking. "No ... " She lowered her fingers. "Can't remember."

"Story of my life. It's *Romeo and Juliet.*"

"The story of your life is a suicidal tragedy we were forced to study in English last year?"

"Not remembering is," he said.

"You remember Shakespeare."

"No, only one line; there's a difference." He smiled. "It's everything else I forget."

"You remember me, right?" she asked.

"You're from *after.*" He turned away, looking out the window as they entered the parking lot of Brunswick High. "I don't remember *before.*"

Justine was one of the first students to stand up when they finally reached the high school, but she stopped a few feet down the aisle. She turned around to look back at him where he sat, still staring out the window.

"Are you joining us for school today, Henry?" she asked when he didn't stand up.

He shrugged. "I was thinking about it."

"Don't take too long." She waved and walked away.

He waved back, but she was long gone. His answering smile melted away when he reached the school, and even the air-conditioning didn't seem to help.

eight

XXX

The house was too quiet when Henry opened the door after school, missing the steady thrum of the central air fighting the good fight against August. No lights illuminated the dark foyer, only weak sunlight struggling through the lead-glass windows high in the walls. The air, thick, heavy, and wet, was difficult to breathe in the heat.

"Dad?" Henry said, still standing in the doorway, though it was hours too early for his father to be home.

Silence.

Henry closed the door, and the light was cut in half while the temperature spiked. The curtains, tattered and torn green fabric that might once have been serviceable, let in slanted rays of weak sunlight, bringing heat more than illumination.

He flipped the switch at the kitchen door. Nothing. He flipped it back and forth once more. Still nothing.

"Again?" he said, his voice quiet in the stillness of the house. He sighed. "Crappy fuse."

In the kitchen he pulled open the drawers, rifling through the random contents—dead batteries and a collection of broken pencils, empty pill bottles. One drawer held hundreds of plastic forks and a single packet of ketchup; another held nothing but pink ribbon tied into miniature bows. Next to an old bag of syringes on top of the fridge, Henry found the flashlight he was looking for, though the batteries were weak when he tested it.

Bigger windows in the laundry room let in more light. A thin door stood behind a rolling cart filled with cleaning supplies, and the wheels squeaked as Henry pulled it out far enough to reach the doorknob. A narrow set of stairs led down into the dark. The air, released on opening, was cool, smelling of age and dust.

The boards creaked on the first wooden step but they held his weight. The flashlight shook with his movements, making the shadows jump around him. Cobwebs came in and out of the light as he turned around, looking for the path to the circuit box to reset the breaker. Shallow footprints were visible in the dust from the last time he'd had to do this, and he followed them through the maze of boxes stored in the basement.

Sweat coated his skin, and kicked-up dust stuck to his

arms and face. The metal door of the circuit box squealed in protest as he slid the latch to open it, and the heavy switch fought against him as he flipped it back into place. The air-conditioner kicked in immediately, a loud roar in the silence.

He'd forgotten to pull the cord to turn on the single bulb hanging from the ceiling; as the batteries of his flashlight died, he was plunged into darkness. Henry shook the flashlight. A weak glow cast shadows but the beam didn't travel very far. He reached his other hand out, back and forth, sensing for boxes, hoping to find the string attached to the light.

Near the circuit breakers? Behind the boxes? Closer to the stairs?

He took a step, his arm swaying back and forth, patting the air as the flashlight died a second death. He shook it, harder and longer, banging it against his hip when it still refused to work.

"Damn it."

The words echoed in the basement as he dropped the flashlight. He took another step, both arms moving to lead the way; the blind leading the blind. His fingers ran into a cobweb, the spider silk sticking to his hand, and he wiped it off on his jeans. Another step and he kicked a stack of boxes. He steadied them with an unsteady hand, continuing to shuffle forward in the darkness.

A hint of light appeared—the sunlight through the windows in the laundry room leaking down the stairs.

Another step, a little lighter, until he could actually see the string hanging down a few feet away.

With a sigh, he pulled it, flooding the basement with light. Henry blinked. Again. The brightness and the dust brought on a sneeze.

He walked back to the circuit breaker to pick up the flashlight. It wasn't there; a trail through the dust showed where it had rolled next to the box he'd kicked. Another inch or so and he would have stepped on it, probably would have tripped and fallen over everything.

As he picked the flashlight up, a feeble beam came out of it and he smiled.

SCRAPBOOK SUPPLIES was written on the bottom box in his father's nearly impossible-to-read scrawl. Henry thought about the photo album upstairs in his room, now battered and torn with use. The mad flipping of pages in his bed late at night when sleep was slow in coming and the pain of forgetting was lessened, somewhat, by the handful of pictures his father had collected for him.

The box on top was heavy, with nothing written on it. He moved it to the side to get to the supplies. Inside, pages of scrapbook paper and little tape dispensers and archival pens were thrown together. He took a few of each. Beneath, he found scissors and stickers, unopened, which had probably come with the paper and pens. He took those as well.

He tried to pick up the other box with his hands partially full. It seemed even heavier than before. In the poor lighting and worse ventilation, dust kicked up and he almost lost his hold on the box.

He sneezed.

The box slipped, reached its tipping point, and fell to the floor. Henry's papers, pens, scissors, and tape went flying.

On its side, the heavy box had opened just enough to make it difficult to pick up again. A single photograph fell out of the small opening, landing on its face. On the back, a woman's hand had written *Frank* above a yellowed date, *March 14*, followed by a year that could have been *1968* or *1963*.

The little boy in the picture was less than five. If Henry squinted in the dim light, it sort of looked like him.

Like Pandora, he opened the box.

There were hundreds of photos, all black-and-white, dated throughout the 1960s and into the 1970s, with the same handwriting. By the time the boy in the photographs was a teen, the resemblance between the stranger and himself was unmistakable.

Frank?

Henry sat in the basement, sneezing, holding the box of snapshots in his lap. One spider had visited to take a look but hadn't stayed for long. A smaller one, barely visible, had scurried back into the box of pictures and not been seen since.

The photos were taken in front of unknown houses; no addresses could be seen or found. No other names appeared even in the pictures where Frank wasn't alone. And in the mid-seventies, the pictures stopped altogether.

Henry dumped the box onto the floor and sifted through them all again, but there was nothing more.

He scooped all the pictures back into the box, gathered up his supplies, and walked to the stairs. On the bottom step he turned around to pull the cord. He froze with his hand on the string and, for the first time, really looked at the boxes lining the maze. Each identical, some with labels, most without.

He walked to the first box and peeked inside.

Blank paper.

Next.

Electrical cords.

Again.

Socks.

And again.

Again.

Another.

Behind him, boxes littered the floor.

Nothing.

Halfway through, with dozens of boxes still to search, he heard the garage door open. He stopped and surveyed the damage he'd done.

Henry jumped over the boxes strewn about and took the narrow stairs two at a time, tugging the string as he ran past. Each step threatened to collapse underneath him and he slipped halfway up. He stopped his fall with his palms and walked the rest of the way, then closed the door and pushed the cart back into place. His pants were dust-covered, cobwebs in his hair and on his shirt.

The clothes went into the washer and he ran his fingers through his hair to dislodge the webs. He hurried up the stairs before his father entered the kitchen. In his room, he went to put on clean clothes and noticed a trail of blood running down his left arm. A splinter from the basement steps stuck out of his palm and small red drops had splattered on the floor.

Henry tried to grab the wood, but his mismatched finger didn't bend far enough. He brought his palm to his mouth and bit down on the splinter. His skin ripped as it tore free. Blood ran over his scar, creating a bracelet of blood on his skin.

A small piece of wood bit into his lip when he spit the splinter out, and he groaned with the sudden pain. He grabbed some tissues to stem the bleeding from his palm. No matter how hard he pressed, his hand didn't hurt at all.

"Why's it so hot?" his father asked when Henry walked downstairs.

"Circuit blew, had to reset the breaker a few minutes ago."

His father looked at the ceiling, where the fan blew warm air around the room. His shoulders slumped and he sighed. He looked at Henry, closed his eyes, and placed the mail on the table unread. Without a word, he walked out of the kitchen.

Henry started to follow, standing at the transition between kitchen tile and hardwood floor, but stopped before he'd taken more than a step or two. A couple of doors stood open, one to a small bathroom and one to an unused office. At the very end of the hall, his father stood before the heavy oak door to the master bedroom.

"Been a long summer, Henry," his father said, not turning around as he rested his hand on the doorknob. He looked back over his shoulder, sighed, and then opened the door.

The air-conditioner had yet to have much of an impact on the heat that had built up in the house. Henry wiped his fingers through his hair, coming away with a few remaining cobwebs, as his father's door locked behind him with a deep thud.

In his room, Henry slid the scrapbook out and opened it up. A page ripped at the bottom when he turned it. Some of the pictures were no longer completely attached to the paper. He gathered his new supplies, switched the light on over his desk, and set to work.

The back of each picture was blank and he had to rely on his father's shaky handwriting in the old scrapbook to keep them in order. One by one, he taped them down on the new paper and copied their captions as neatly as possible. When he was done, he started at the beginning, looking at each photograph of himself and trying to remember who he was.

William locked the door with a deep thud as the deadbolt slid home. He stood there for a long time, hand still gripping the knob, his breathing ragged and uneven, trying to find the strength to move. There was nothing there, no energy left. No motivation to do anything beyond collapse to the ground, curl up into a ball, and stay there until his heart finally gave out.

He shook his head, thin gray hair fluttering in front of his eyes. Reaching up, he grabbed a few of the remaining strands and pulled them out. The sharp pain brought relief from the lethargy and he ripped out another small handful until he was able to move from the door to the window. As he walked he let the hair fall from his fingers, landing on the dusty floor to join the rest.

Pushing aside the thick curtains just enough to peek out, he looked at the backyard, studying the way the shadows crawled across the barren dirt as the sun began to set. He stood there, a single trail of blood running down the side of his face where he'd pulled too hard, until the moon cast a pale light over the island.

He smiled, letting the curtain fall closed. "Time to hunt," he said, his voice soft as he wiped the blood away.

Possible Second Head Trauma Victim Discovered in Brunswick

Brunswick, GA—August 18, 2009: Barely two months after Sylvia Foote's death was ruled a homicide, the Glynn County Sheriff's office has announced the possibility of a connected victim. Derrick Fischer, 31, was found off Route 17, half buried along the side of the road. "Along with the state forensics lab, FLETC, and the Brunswick Police Department, we have assigned a task force to look into these unfortunate events to determine if they're related," said Assistant District Attorney Brian Winters when asked if Fischer and Foote had any similarities.

Preliminary autopsy results on Fischer, according to unofficial sources, show that death was, as in the Foote case, allegedly caused by blunt force trauma, though what is believed to be post-mortem injuries make an exact cause of death difficult to determine at this time.

FLETC houses multi-departmental government training facilities for all branches of law enforcement throughout the United States. To assist with this investigation, Winters has announced that a liaison officer has been assigned by FLETC to coordinate with local police as a symbol of the concern they have for the community. "As of this time," Winters said, "we will gratefully accept any assistance and do not believe there are any additional concerns in regards to the current matter that would necessitate FLETC involvement."

Major Daniel Johnson of the United States Army Criminal Investigation Command (USACIDC) in Fort Belvoir, VA, who is in Brunswick as a trainer at FLETC, has been assigned to act as liaison but was unavailable for comment.

“Comedy of Errors” Leads to Temporary “Escape” for GRPH Patients

Brunswick, GA—August 18, 2009: During a recent field trip by residents of the minimum-security wing of the Georgia Regional Psychiatric Hospital in Brunswick to the Jacksonville Zoo, several patients were temporarily reported missing. Despite repeated calls for greater security due to previous errors in the intake process at the state-run facility, this is the first incident reported where convicted patients have allegedly not been under direct supervision.

“These non-violent offenders are no danger to the community,” said Dr. Jason Rapp, Chief of Staff for the hospital, after rumors of the temporary escape were reported in the *Savannah Morning News*. “At no time were the patients thought to have escaped. All current residents of the hospital are present and accounted for.”

Margaret Saville, PhD
St. Simons Island, Glynn County, GA
Tuesday, August 18, 2009
Patient: Henry Franks
(DOB: November 19, 1992)

Henry crossed his legs, pressing his palms into his thighs to keep from scratching. Despite the air-conditioning, sweat coated his skin. He pushed down and sighed.

"The heat index is over one hundred, Henry," Dr. Saville said. "You don't actually have to wear pants."

He looked at her and moved his hands out to the side. "You've seen my legs, Doctor."

She nodded. "Still, maybe something lighter than denim, at least?"

Henry shrugged.

"Just a thought."

"It'll be cooler soon."

"November isn't actually soon," she said. "How's school?"

He shrugged again. "It's school."

"Two word answers aren't really much better than one, Henry."

Is my father's name Frank Franks or are the pictures of me? But he didn't ask that particular question out loud. *If Franks isn't my father's real name, what's my name?* But he didn't ask that question either.

"A lot more police outside the hospital," he said.

"Excuse me?"

"This morning. On the bus, when we drove past, it was surrounded."

"Do you always notice the hospital?"

Henry shook his head, hiding behind his hair. "It's big."

"Does it bother you?"

"People who can't remember who they are get sent there," he said, the words bitten off and harsh.

"Is that what you're afraid of?"

"Would it help?" he asked.

"What?"

"Going there; would it help?"

Dr. Saville tapped her pen against the pad, her head cocked to the side. "The Georgia Regional Psychiatric Hospital is for criminals who have been admitted for detention and treatment, Henry. Not for teenage boys who survived accidents."

"It's still big," he said with a half-smile.

"Yes, it is," she said. "Any dreams lately?"

"My dad switched the dosages around on me," he said. "I don't dream as much now."

"Is that a good thing?"

"I miss Elizabeth," he said and closed his eyes.

"Henry?"

"In my dreams now, I don't recognize anyone. Or any place. Like they're not my dreams."

"Maybe they're people and places you've forgotten?"

He pressed his hands into his legs. "I don't think so."

"Why not?"

"They call me Victor."

"That's not really your name, Henry."

"That's what they tell me." He smiled and then shrugged. "How would I know?"

"Have you talked to your father about any of this?"

"We don't ... well, no," he said. "That's not what we do."

"What?"

"Talk."

"About this?" she asked.

"About anything. I don't think he likes me very much."

Dr. Saville's pen stopped and she looked up at him over her notebook. "Why do you say that?"

"Mom died."

"That's it?"

Henry wiped his eyes. "I should have died too. It's been hard on him, I guess."

"You lived, Henry."

"I forget what my mother looked like as soon as I stop looking at her picture, like she's a stranger and the photo came in the frame from the store."

"Post-traumatic stress and retrograde amnesia,

that's what we've been working on," Dr. Saville said. "It's a process."

"It's not working."

"It takes time."

"I can't remember her name."

"Henry." She stretched her hand out, resting long fingers against the arm of his chair for just a moment.

He slammed his head back, striking the fabric with a dull thud, and then looked at her through the fall of his hair with red eyes. His breath came hard and fast, hyperventilating. "I can't remember *me*."

"Take deep breaths."

"I can't."

"Henry!" Dr. Saville reached his side in one step, and then moved back as his arms flailed out.

"I—" He rocked back and forth, banging his head against the chair. "I—" He blinked, over and over again, the motions erratic and strained as he clawed at his skin, leaving faint trails of blood behind.

"Deep breaths, Henry."

Dr. Saville knelt in front of him and held his hands down after he drew blood from the scar on his wrist. He shook like a wild animal cornered after a fight; his thrashing banged his skull against her chin. "Breathe, Henry."

His heart hammered against his ribs and he couldn't catch his breath.

"Breathe." She took a deep breath. "Slow, Henry, remember?"

When he looked up at her, a trail of blood ran from her bottom lip, and the bright red caught his attention more than her words.

"Breathe," she said before she took another deep breath. "Count to ten, Henry."

And he did.

"Again."

Together, they held their breath. Inhale. Exhale. Again. Until she released him and he collapsed into the chair.

"You need to practice your relaxation techniques more."

"You're bleeding," he said, pointing at her chin.

Dr. Saville grabbed a tissue and wiped her face.

Henry hung his head between his knees, letting his hair fall back in front of his eyes. "I'm sorry."

"It's all right, Henry," she said. "Are you feeling better now?"

"I miss Elizabeth."

"Why?"

"We talked."

"About?"

"I can't remember. Just stuff."

"Is there anyone else you talk to?"

"You." Henry sat up, brushing the hair away,

trying to forget the brief image of her eating breakfast with his father. He wanted to ask her about it but the words caught inside his throat and all that came out was a hiss.

"Anyone else?"

"No."

"Don't you talk with Justine?" she asked.

"On the bus."

"That's someone."

He shrugged. "She does most of the talking."

"Do you know that you smile when you talk about her?"

Henry pulled his hair in front of his face and then turned away. "So?"

"You don't smile when you talk about Elizabeth."

"So?" He took a deep breath, held it and counted to ten on his fingers, then released it.

"So, Henry," she said. "Better?"

Who's Henry? But like all the others, that question was silent as well.

"Maybe," he said.

The door opened up to the heat, and where the outside met the air-conditioning inside was a weather system unto itself; moist, hot, and too thick to inhale. The bright sun burned off the blacktop and his sunglasses did little to dull the impact. A headache started almost immediately.

His father waited in the parking lot, engine running to keep cool, and Henry slid in as quickly as possible.

"How'd it go?" his father asked as he pulled onto Demere Road.

Henry turned up the air-conditioning and then rested his head back on the seat, eyes closed. "Fine."

"Henry?"

He opened one eye, peering at his father through the hair falling in front of his face. He sighed. "It's a process."

"Did Dr. Saville say anything?"

"About?"

"You?" his father asked.

"No."

Henry pulled at the collar of his shirt, closed his eyes, and looked away.

His father turned the car into Harrison Pointe and parked in front of the house. "I'll be working late again. Don't forget to do your homework."

"Fine," Henry said before grabbing his backpack and opening the door.

Inside, he waited until his father drove away before rushing down the fragile wooden stairs into the basement, stepping carefully to avoid the splinters that were poking out of the old lumber.

He pulled the cord but the weak light failed to reach the corners. The mess he'd left the day before was gone. Stacks of cardboard boxes lined the room, with well-swept and cobweb-free aisles between them.

Henry ran to the circuit box.

The *SCRAPBOOK SUPPLIES* box sat nearby, but when he lifted the box on top, it was far too light to still be filled with ancient photographs. A few scraps of archival paper and stickers rattled around, but there were no pictures.

One by one, he searched through the rest of the boxes.

It took him hours, but by the time he was done he'd failed to find the photographs in any of them.

Drenched in sweat, he climbed up the stairs, put the cart back in place, and collapsed into a chair, resting his head on the kitchen table next to his backpack. A branch scraped across the side of the house like fingernails on a blackboard. Henry jumped up and crossed to the sink to look into the backyard. Light filtered through the leaves, casting fluid shadows that seemed to move with the breeze. Spanish moss hung, still and silent, from the towering oaks, not moving, and when he looked closer there was no wind at all.

Henry walked down the hallway, to the door to the master bedroom. He put his ear to the wood, trying to hear something from the other side, but there was nothing but the hum of the air-conditioning. Just to be safe, he knocked. The sound was loud and seemed to linger in the too-warm air. The knob was cool in his hand but, even though it turned, it didn't open the door.

"Damn," he said, before slapping his palm into the door. It tingled, but just a little, and there was no pain from hitting the wood.

In his father's office across the hall, Henry pulled out drawers, looking for the photographs of Frank, but the drawers were empty. Dust coated the top of the desk and the shelves were bare. When he rolled the desk chair out to look underneath, the metal wheels squealed in protest and left tracks through the dust on the floor. Behind him, his own footprints stood out in stark relief, and only when he was in the hallway again did he relax enough to breathe.

Henry ate dinner alone in the empty house and then went upstairs to his room. He surfed around the Internet but gave up after only a minute or two. The sun was still bright in the August sky and he watched it crawl toward the horizon. In his lap, his dark index finger idly scratched at the scar on his wrist.

He took a deep breath and then unfolded the piece of paper hidden beneath his pillbox. When he grasped the pen, it slipped out of his fingers and, try as he might, he couldn't get his mismatched index finger to hold on to it. With it squeezed in his fist, he added *Frank* to the list of names.

Henry went back downstairs when he heard his father return home, but by the time he got to the kitchen, the room was empty again. He looked down the hall toward the master bedroom. Beneath the door, a sliver of light glowed.

He took a step onto the hardwood floor and stopped. The corridor seemed longer than it had when he was still standing on the tile of the kitchen. The floor squeaked with each step, a high-pitched echo of his heartbeat, until he finally reached the door. Up close, it was carved, the dark wood etched with faint patterns that matched the wainscoting. He took a deep breath, thinking of all the questions left unasked. Unanswered.

He knocked.

"Dad?"

Silence, save for the constant hum of the air-conditioning. Henry tried the knob but it didn't turn. He rested his finger on the deadbolt lock above it.

"Dad?"

He knocked, again.

At his feet, the light from under the door disappeared without a sound.

Henry sat at his desk, the house an empty shell around him despite the presence, somewhere, of his silent father. The summer sun had finally given way to night, cooling his room almost enough to notice. Still, the central air and ceiling fan worked non-stop.

Next to his monitor a generic plastic box divided into sections held his medicine. *AM* and *PM* and each day of the week were scrawled on pieces of masking tape on top. He flicked his finger through the *Tuesday PM* pills but couldn't find the energy to take them.

He closed the lid and sat there unmoving, staring at the screen saver on his computer defining words he couldn't remember as he re-opened the pillbox.

He was still sitting there when he fell asleep, medicine untaken in his hand.

"Daddy!"

Elizabeth comes running up to me, flinging herself into my arms. Her weight is a comfort against me as I swing her around. Just a child, she still shrieks with glee, making funny propeller noises as she flies.

Around us, petals fall off the trees like leaves in autumn, falling in patterns to the ground. They smell of earth and roses and I know they'd taste of ice cream.

"Chocolate," Elizabeth says, her tiny hand tucked in mine as we wait in line.

"One scoop?"

"Two," she says.

I have to use more pressure than I expect to drag the spoon through the vat of ice cream, scraping up a small ball that rattles around her cup, making odd metallic creaking noises like artificial bones held together with pins and prayer. The sun burns down, melting the ice cream into drinkable joy.

Elizabeth slurps and smiles and holds my hand as we wander through the empty park. Red and golden leaves crunch underfoot.

"I've got a secret," she says.

Ice cream has given her a chocolate mustache and she licks it off. Her pigtails are coming undone and her dress is communion pretty; a small red poppy trails a Memorial Day ribbon on her chest.

"A secret?" I scoop her up in my arms and she squeals with delight.

"Daddy!" She laughs as I swing her around, making airplane noises.

We land, walking hand in hand down a deserted airport concourse. She tugs us forward, pulling me faster and faster until we're running, flying over the moving walkways and abandoned luggage to our gate.

"See?" she asks, pointing toward the two people sleeping in the hard orange chairs. On the TV above them, all the flights have been cancelled.

"This is your secret, Elizabeth?" I ask.

"Your secret, Daddy." She smiles. "I promised you I wouldn't tell anyone. Not even Mommy."

"My secret?"

She pushes me toward the gate, closer to the people lying there. At first, I think they're Martians, their skin is so purple. They aren't breathing.

Humans. Beaten so badly as to bruise their skin darker than grapes.

"Elizabeth?" I call her name, spinning around and around in the empty airport. "Elizabeth!"

But there's no one there.

Just a white dress lying on the floor, a growing red stain like blood from where I'd pinned the poppy on her.

On the TV set above my head, there is suddenly one more cancelled flight.

Henry was awake long before the alarm; early enough to lie on his bed and watch the room lighten as the sun broke through the leaves outside his window. He moved his hand to the table and crawled it toward the clock until he could turn the beeping off. Then he rubbed his eyes but failed to banish sleep or the half-formed memories of his dream.

His heart beat too slowly, and it seemed to be more of a conscious decision to breathe than it should be. The thought, *inhale/exhale*, repeated itself.

"Breathe, Henry," he said.

He rolled out of bed and rubbed his hands over his face as he walked to the bathroom. His fingers came away wet and red. He stared at his bloody palms. In his reflection in the mirror above the sink, his nose was bleeding and he'd rubbed blood over the bottom half of his face.

When he was finished washing up, his nose was sore, his eyes puffy, and his pale skin seemed translucent where he'd scraped it raw with the towel. The snooze alarm sounded as he was about to get in the shower. He dragged himself back to his room to shut it off and collapsed onto the edge of the bed, head in his hands. His nose started bleeding again.

"Breathe."

Henry walked to the end of the Harrison Pointe subdivision to wait for the bus. The sidewalks were cracking where the roots of the trees were trying to escape and Spanish moss hung so far down that he had to duck under it at times, but he still managed to get some tangled in his hair.

At the bus stop he stood alone, the only student not wearing shorts. He kept his eyes on the ground until a pair of sandals appeared, pink-painted toes sticking out. Henry glanced up, far enough for his vision to travel halfway over long tan legs, a small scab healing on the right knee, before returning to her toes.

"Who died?" Justine asked.

"What?"

"You look terrible," she said. "Well, all in black as always, so maybe you're in perpetual mourning. But, seriously, new heights of goth, very impressive."

He looked up at her, meeting her gaze. His eyes still red from rubbing and his pale skin glistening with sweat, he swallowed whatever he had been about to say when he saw her smile.

"Henry?" she said. Her hand reached out but she didn't touch him, then she took a step closer and dropped her voice, her smile melting away in the heat. "I'm sorry, *did* someone die?"

He shook his head. "No. Just..." He lowered his eyes. "Just a dream."

The bus pulled to the curb with a hydraulic groan, the door opening on hinges in need of oiling, and they filed on board. Justine sat down in the seat in front of him as the bus pulled away.

"I'm a good listener," she said. "Well, I'm a better talker, but..."

Henry rested his head on the window, the glass cool to the touch despite the heat, and looked at her. The bra strap once again matched her tank top, blue this time. "You don't match."

"What?" she asked.

"Your toes. They don't match."

She laughed, and he could feel other people on the bus looking at them. "I matched yesterday. Didn't you notice?"

He shook his head.

"You're blushing," she said. "You noticed."

"Sorry." He smiled, and then looked out the window at the imposing bulk of the Georgia Regional Psychiatric

Hospital. The towers at each corner of the barbed wire fence cast a shadow over the trees lining the road.

"Who died?" she asked. "In your dream?"

"I don't know." Henry shook his head before looking back at her. "Strangers."

"You didn't know them?"

"I can't remember."

"Your dream?" she asked.

"No. If I knew them before."

She turned around in her seat, resting her arms on the back. "That's what the doctor's for, right?"

"So I'm okay with not remembering."

"Are you?"

He shrugged.

"What do you do when you're there?" she asked.

"Talk."

"You? You never talk."

"I'm talking to you."

She smiled. Pink lips tilted upwards, honey eyes sparkled in the summer sun, the whole framed by brown hair pulled back into a ponytail. Stray strands had escaped and curled down along her neck, sticking to her skin in the heat.

Inhale/Exhale, he thought. *Breathe.*

Just breathe.

eleven

XXX

The school bus baked all day in the August sun. Even with the windows opened, it was still baking when the driver pulled into the parking lot to wait for students. Dressed for summer, they placed sheets of paper on the benches before sitting down on the hot vinyl seats.

As Henry walked down the aisle, Bobby was sitting in Justine's seat, his arm resting on the back of the bench. The bus slowly filled up and Henry briefly tried to lower his window but gave up without success.

"Justine," Bobby called down the aisle. "I saved a seat for you."

Henry looked up; even from a distance he could see her eyes widen as she saw Bobby sitting in her seat. She stopped for a moment as he patted the plastic cushion, then shook her head.

"Bobby, you're incorrigible," she said. "That's Latin for 'incapable of being corrected.'"

"Is that a good thing?" he asked, still patting the seat.

Behind her, a couple of students were backing up in the aisle.

"No," she said, a bright smile taking some, but not much, of the sting out of the word. "It's not." She took a step down the aisle and stopped at Henry's seat. She looked back at Bobby and then turned to Henry.

"I sweat more just looking at you," she said. "Move over."

Henry slid to the side as Justine put down a protective notebook paper barrier between plastic and skin.

"Thanks," she said.

Bobby swung around in his seat, leaning over toward Justine. "You'd rather sit with Scarface?" he asked.

Henry tried to squeeze even further into the window, but Justine simply laughed. "That's the best you could come up with, Bobby? You might want to work on that. And, if you need to ask, I was raised to believe that the choice of where to sit was mine."

Bobby looked from Justine to Henry, then grabbed his backpack and walked to the back of the bus with the other football players. Justine waved goodbye but he didn't see it. As the diesel engine coughed to life, she giggled.

"Scarface?" she asked, looking at Henry. "I'm sorry, he's a

jerk sometimes, but he's not as rude as he tries to pretend to be. He does have a slight problem with persistence, though."

Henry shrugged, and then brushed the hair out of his face. "Is that a bad thing?"

"I'm not allowed to date," Justine said. "Not football players, not pre-med students at Coastal College, not twenty-something teachers or the guy that sells pretzels at the mall." She laughed. "Well, I'm exaggerating about most of that, but still." She smiled. "My parents have made it perfectly clear that I'm not to date until I'm a senior, and then only in groups, if I keep my grades up. So persistence isn't necessarily a bad thing. Though, even if I could date, it wouldn't be Bobby Dixon. But it is rather pointless, don't you think?"

He opened his mouth but nothing came out, so he shrugged again and simply closed his mouth.

"So," she said, "you never really told me about your dream from last night."

"What?" he asked, still trying to absorb everything else she'd said. Too many words in too little time, leading to such a random statement.

"You looked terrible all day, didn't even say hi when you shuffled past me in the halls," she said. "Not that you noticed I was there. Don't you walk into walls staring at the ground all day?"

"I don't..."

"I can't really picture you talking with a shrink," Justine added with a smile. "You don't say much."

"Is it my turn to talk yet?"

She laughed, then nodded. "Your turn."

"No one-word answers," he said. "It's on a sign in her office."

"That's a start, at least."

"I waved."

"When?"

The blue straps of her tank top were wide enough to hide her bra, while leaving long stretches of tan skin exposed up her neck and down her shoulders. Beaded with sweat, she glistened in the sunlight. Henry ran his fingers through his hair, unable, as always, to figure out where to rest his eyes.

"When?" she asked again, leaning into him with the turns the bus was making on its journey home.

"After second period. You walked by me."

"How do you know?"

"Pink nail polish." He looked up in time to watch a smile crawl across her face.

"What will you do when I change colors?"

He shrugged. "I check in the mornings."

She turned to face him, her smile as wide as he'd ever seen it. A slight blush spread across her skin and for a moment he not only forgot to breathe, he forgot how.

"You had a dream?" she asked, the words barely spoken out loud. He found himself leaning closer to her to hear.

"Dr. Saville says it's a part of the process," he said. "I have these dreams, about people I don't know, places I've never been."

"Are they from before the accident?"

"I don't think so," he said.

"Why not?"

"Ever have the same dream over and over again?" he asked.

She nodded.

"Seem real, don't they?"

"Sometimes."

"Mine are always like that."

"Last night?"

"I have a daughter," he said, hiding behind his hair. "Her name's Elizabeth."

Her mouth dropped open and for a moment she didn't speak at all. "For real?" she asked, her voice quiet.

"In the dream."

"Aren't you my age?"

"Sixteen," he said, moving his hair out of the way to look at her.

"How do you know she's your daughter?"

Henry sighed. "She calls me Daddy."

"Well, now I know why you don't think it's from before the accident."

"Just felt so real. Then I woke up." Henry turned and looked out the window as they passed the hospital. Police cars blocked the entrance where a local news van was parked, the antenna stabbing into the sky.

"It's not as creepy as it looks," she said, her voice soft.

"What?"

"The hospital." She pointed out the window as they left the facility behind. "My dad's cousin is in there." She shook her head with a quick smile. "I've only met him once; he's a lot older. Used to live in Waycross, I think. He's been there as long as I can remember."

"I'm sorry," Henry said, turning to face her.

She shrugged. "My dad visits him every so often. He dragged me along once. Wasn't as bad as I thought it would be from all the barbed wire, you know?"

The bus came to a stop and Henry followed Justine down the steps to the street.

"Almost as good as a breeze," she said while swinging around in a circle, her hair flying out around her face.

"Almost."

"Do you dream about dead people a lot?"

"Lately."

"Been in the news."

"What?" he asked.

"Dead people. Lots of dead people around town."

They stopped where the low metal gate swung open to the walkway to his house. It wouldn't stay shut; the hinges were rusty and the white paint was flaking off like dandruff. Since there was no fence anywhere else around the front half of the property, it didn't much matter, really, if the lonely gate was closed or not.

"Sweet dreams, Henry," she said, and rested her hand on his arm for a moment before she walked toward her house.

"Thanks," he said; then, louder, so she could hear, he said it again, standing on the sidewalk watching her walk away.

Hinges squealed as the door opened. William jumped at the sound, turning around just as Henry walked into the kitchen. The hint of a smile on his son's face faded as they stared at each other. William looked down at the bloodstains on his work clothes and tried to hide them behind his hands.

"Sorry," he said as he pushed past Henry, pulling his consultation jacket off as he walked, leaving bloody fingerprints on the white sleeves as he slid out of it.

"Dad?" his son said, the word distant and barely more than a whisper through the pounding of his heartbeat in his ears.

He looked over his shoulder as he fumbled with the keys, trying to slide the right one into the deadbolt. "Didn't have time to clean up after work," he called as the key finally slid home.

He slammed the door shut behind him, the echo storming through the house like thunder. William threw the coat into the corner and ran to the bathroom. Heavy curtains covered the window in there, as well, and he was rushing too much to turn on the light. In the dark shadows he turned the hot water on and began scraping at his hands to scrub off the blood.

The water steamed and turned red as he held his hands underneath it. He scrubbed, over and over, rubbing his hands together. His fingers trembled as he tried to get all the blood off. In the darkness it was difficult to see if they were clean or not, so he just kept scrubbing.

Tears fell into the sink, mixing with the blood as he stood there, boiling his hands until they were sterile. Still, he didn't stop until the water turned cold.

Discovery of Two Additional Bodies Leads to Calls for a Town Hall Meeting

Saint Simons Island, GA—August 19, 2009: In what has become an all-too familiar scene this summer, Glynn County Sheriff's Officers were called to the beach beneath the village pier where an early morning fisherman discovered two bodies behind a piling.

Charles Bensen, 63, and his wife, Gertrude, 59, residents of Manchester, NH, were visiting family when they were reported missing earlier this week.

Preliminary autopsy reports list blunt force trauma as the preliminary cause of death.

"At this time, it would be counterproductive to speculate on any connections between this unfortunate occurrence and any other ongoing investigations," said Staci Carr, District Attorney of Glynn County.

"We will continue to follow all leads and value all contributions from the community," said Major Daniel Johnson of FLETC as they sealed off the beach.

The Bensens are the fifth and sixth deaths in Glynn County this summer, all allegedly from blunt force trauma. While preliminary research has not shown any connection between the victims—Sylvia Foote, Crayton Mission, Paul Wislon, Derrick Fischer, and the Bensons—police spokesperson Carmella Rawls has issued a "No comment" when asked for further details from the official autopsy reports.

Brunswick mayor Jim Monroe has announced a press conference and town hall meeting for August 20, 2009 at 7:00 PM in the Glynn Academy auditorium to discuss recent events. All interested parties are invited to attend.

Margaret Saville, PhD
St. Simons Island, Glynn County, GA
Thursday, August 20, 2009
Patient: Henry Franks
(DOB: November 19, 1992)

The leaves of the palm tree, brushing listlessly against the window, were brown and dying. One sprinkler head peeked out above the dry grass but no water shot forth and patches of dirt had broken through. Henry turned back to the doctor, his fingers resting on his wrist, trailing the scar.

"Henry." Her pen hung like the sword of Damocles over her legal pad. "I was wondering if you ever sleepwalk."

He shrugged.

"Are you still tired when you wake up?" she asked.

"Sometimes," he said.

"When?"

He looked out the window, then pulled his hair down in front of his eyes.

"Henry?"

"I don't know."

"Can you try to remember for me?" she asked.

"Will that help?"

"Maybe. You might be having blackouts and not even realizing it."

"Better," Henry said with a shrug, "to ask Elizabeth."

"Elizabeth?"

"Or Victor."

"They're not real, Henry."

"I know. I'm forgetful, not crazy."

"Amnesia doesn't mean that. It's a process to remember," she said. "Your brain is still trying to understand the accident and, perhaps, it's using your dreams to help with that."

"There was an accident," he said, each word its own sentence, distinct and harsh.

"Yes."

"I should have died."

"You remember that?"

He shook his head, hair flying away from his face, and his eyes couldn't stay still. "No."

"No?"

"My dad told me, 'There was an accident.' I remember him telling me, about the rain, the construction; I should have died." Henry slumped down in the chair, his hands falling open on the seat. One deep breath after another. He held the last one, counting to ten, mouthing the numbers. "There was an accident. I should have died."

"And?"

"There was an accident."

"Henry?"

"I should have died."

He slumped there, moving only enough to breathe. His eyes twitched to the side, the rapid tics out of place in his pale motionless face.

"There was an accident."

"Henry," she said, walking across the office to sit on the couch next to him. "It's Dr. Saville. Can you breathe for me?"

He took one long shuddering breath and closed his eyes.

"Henry?"

"I had another dream."

His hand flopped to the couch between them, as though it wasn't even attached to an arm. The scar wrapped around the wrist glistened with sweat. The back of the hand had a dusting of fine pale hairs that almost reached the scar. Above the scar, up his forearm, dark hair stuck to the skin in the heat.

"Anyone you know?" she asked.

"Elizabeth."

"No one else?"

"Strangers," he said.

"Dead?"

He nodded. A wall of bangs fell into his eyes and he left them there.

"Who?"

"I don't know."

"You didn't recognize them at all?" she asked.

"No."

"Did Elizabeth?"

"She told me she had a secret," he said.

"A secret?"

"They're always dead."

"Elizabeth's secrets?"

"She didn't do it," he said.

"Did she tell you that?" she asked.

"Doesn't have to. I know."

"Why?"

"She didn't know them."

"Henry?"

"Just a dream, right?" He raised his head, looking at her.

"Your nose is bleeding." Dr. Saville crossed the room to get a tissue, but when she turned back around Henry was standing right behind her. She stumbled against the foot of her chair.

He reached out his blond-haired hand to steady her, leaving a bloody print on her sleeve. Trails of blood had streaked around his mouth and down his chin; drops splattered on his shirt.

"It's the meds. They make my nose bleed." He smiled at her, his white teeth sharp in a sea of red. "You okay?"

Dr. Saville pulled her arm out of his grasp. "Here," she handed him the box of tissues. "For your nose."

He sat down, head back, and counted his breaths. "Just a dream," he said, talking to the ceiling.

"Does she have any other secrets, Henry?"

He shrugged and then looked up at her. "I think more people are going to die."

Blood had stained his teeth, but his nose had stopped bleeding. Dried red flakes remained on his lips and chin when he smiled.

"Henry?"

"There was an accident," he whispered, the words barely audible. "I should have died." He closed his eyes and the silence stretched out as he took one deep breath after another.

The alarm shattered the quiet. Henry stood up, next to Dr. Saville as she dropped the pad down on the desk. It landed next to a folded-over copy of the *Brunswick News*. He could only see half of the full-color photograph of police cars beneath a banner headline about the two bodies found the day before. The top sheet of paper on the pad, beneath Henry's name and the date, was blank except for the one drop of blood that had fallen on it.

Justine was in his seat when he climbed up the steps onto the bus. As Henry walked down the plastic runner, her mouth fell open and, as he sat down next to her, she pushed it closed with her index finger.

"You own a *white* shirt?" She smiled before her mouth fell open again in mock surprise. "Really? White? I'm shocked."

"Does it ruin my look?"

"You have a look?" She laughed. "I guess shorts would have been too much to ask for?"

"I—" He looked at her. Her bare legs were tan and a stark contrast to his dark jeans. A green tank top hid her bra strap but little else, and he swallowed before looking away. "I never wear shorts."

"What do you swim in?"

"I don't know how to swim."

"Is that another one of those things you don't remember? Maybe you used to swim? How would you know?"

"My father made a scrapbook," he said. "With a bunch of pictures of me from before the accident." Henry ran his fingers through his hair, but it fell back down in front of his eyes anyway.

"Any with you in shorts?"

He shrugged. "I don't know, never looked."

"Can I see?"

"Me in shorts?"

"Well, now that you mention it," she said before shaking her head. "No, the scrapbook."

"Why?"

Justine looked up, half-turning to face him. Her fingers, with their pale pink nail polish, drummed against the seat between them. She smiled. "To help?"

He looked at her, studying the warmth of her smile, the depth of her eyes as she faced him. He took a deep breath and smiled back. "I found some pictures in the basement the other day."

"Of you?"

"No. I don't know. They looked like me," he said. "But these were old, black-and-white."

"Did they remind you of anything?"

"I think maybe they're of my dad."

"So?" she asked.

"When I went back to look at them, they were gone."

"Gone?"

"The basement was cleaned up and the pictures were missing."

"Maybe your dad has them," Justine said. "Have you asked him?"

"I tried, but I don't see him very often, really." Henry smiled. "I live the perfect teenage life, no parents." The smile faded. "Kinda sucks."

She rested her fingers on his arm, right above the scar, as the bus pulled into the high school. The movement slid her strap down her shoulder.

"You match again," Henry said. Even through her tan, she blushed.

They walked off the bus and into school together until her friends called her away. Still, she lingered next to him a moment longer before leaving. His scar, which she'd almost touched, didn't itch at all.

After eating lunch, Henry left the cafeteria and headed for the library, hoping to catch Justine before she finished studying. As he passed the lab he almost ran into the new science teacher, but someone reached out for him, grabbing his arm and pulling him out of the way.

"Trying to kill another teacher, Scarface?" Bobby said.

"What?" Henry tried to shrug out of Bobby's grip, but the much-larger football player held him easily.

"You live on the island, don't you?" Bobby asked. "Lots of dead bodies piling up out there. I think I might need to start gathering some pitchforks and villagers."

Henry squirmed, but Bobby just pushed him harder into the lockers. The hall was empty now that the teacher had gone in to the lab. "Just let me go."

"Oh, and about Justine? She's cute," Bobby said. "Out of your league, though, sorry about that." He smiled and pushed Henry away, sending him to the floor.

Henry picked himself up but Bobby was already walking into the library. He looked through the library window long enough to see Justine turn away from Bobby, but he was too far away to hear what she said.

"Out of your league too," Henry said with a smile, running his fingers over the scar on his wrist.

Officials at Town Hall Meeting Warn of Suspected Serial Killings

Brunswick, GA—August 21, 2009: Mayor Jim Monroe appeared with Carmella Rawls of the Brunswick Police Department and Major Daniel Johnson of FLETC at a press conference at Glynn Academy in Brunswick on Thursday evening to discuss the investigation into what is being called a suspicious series of murders in Glynn County. While few details were given, some guidelines were provided by the Mayor to increase public safety. The main recommendation was to utilize the Buddy System by traveling in pairs when possible.

"This is not a time for panic or overreaction," Mayor Monroe said. "This is a time for the community to come together and resolve to rededicate ourselves to preserving the safe, family-friendly environment that makes Brunswick and the Golden Isles such a wonderful place to live and visit."

"I'm confident in the resiliency of the people of Glynn County and in the resources which have been allocated to this situation," Mayor Monroe stated at the end of the press conference. "I urge everyone to support our community and our local businesses by continuing to enjoy the beautiful summer we have been having."

XXX

“Any plans for the weekend?” Justine asked as they walked off the bus.

“Air-conditioning. You?”

“Not going to the football game tonight?”

Henry slid his hands into the pockets of his jeans and shook his head. “Wasn’t planning on it. Don’t really know what I’m going to do.”

“Well,” she said, “I was thinking today.”

“Is that a good thing?”

“Yes.” Her ponytail bobbed with her smile. “It’s a good thing. I’d like to help.”

“Help?” Henry asked.

“The pictures, in your basement.”

"What about them?"

"Want help finding them?"

The front door stuck when he tried to open it and it took a push or two to work the key. A welcome rush of cold air blew out and Henry fumbled for the light switch.

"Now I know where you get your style," Justine said, looking around the entranceway.

"My style?"

"All dark and moody. You dress like your house."

"It was like this when we moved in, I think. Blame the people who lived here before." Henry matched her laugh. "Though it is a little depressing in here."

"No wonder you're seeing a shrink," she said, pushing against his forearm as they walked. When he didn't respond, she said, "That was a joke, you know?"

In the kitchen, with a couple more windows and a little more light, he looked at her. "I know."

"Where are we going?"

"Through here." He led the way into the laundry room. "Wasn't a particularly funny one, though."

"What?"

"Your joke," he said, hair once more falling into his face. He brushed it aside and then pulled out the rolling cart. "Perhaps 'the interior designer was suffering from Prozac withdrawal' would have been funnier."

Justine shook her head, ponytail flying behind her. "Mine was better than that."

"I'll think of something."

"Probably not."

Henry opened the door and picked up the flashlight he'd left on the cart, complete with fresh batteries. "The pull cord's down here. Watch your step."

"I have a basement too, you know," she said, closing the door behind them and walking past him down the stairs.

The hanging bulb cast a weak light over the piles of boxes.

"Back here." Henry led the way through the basement. "This box, it had pictures in it." He flipped the flaps open and shone the flashlight into the empty corners. "The next day they were gone. I searched everywhere but couldn't find them. Everything was cleaned up; even the spider webs had been swept away."

"'So, Justine, what did you do today?'" she said. "'Well, Mom, I went into the creepy house next door and all the spiders were gone. It was just terrible.'"

"You only think you're funny."

"Nope, I have a certificate and everything. It's official; I'm funny." She stood there looking up at him. "I'm sorry. I can stop if you'd like."

"Really?"

"Well," she said, a smile teasing the edges of her lips, "I could try to stop. For you."

He turned and worked his way to the opposite end of

the room, picking a box at random to open. “I think you’re funny,” he said, not looking at her.

She popped her head up from the other side of the room. “I heard that!”

“Not deaf, but definitely funny.”

“I’m sorry, did you say something?” She opened a box, closed it, opened the next, working her way toward him. “Someone sick?”

“Why?”

She pulled out an unopened box of face masks. “There are lots of medical supplies in here.”

“My dad’s a doctor,” he said.

“See, that’s why you’re seeing a shrink.”

“Still not funny.”

“What kind of doctor?” She closed the box and moved on to the next one.

“Forensics.”

“Like, with dead people?”

“I guess so.”

“This really is the creepy house. Does your shrink have an opening for me?”

They worked their way from one end of the basement to the other, box to box, until they met in the middle.

“Why would he hide them?” she asked.

Henry rubbed his eyes. Sweat beaded his skin and his palms were moist; his scars itched in the heat. He closed the last box with a sigh.

“I don’t know.”

“Maybe he was just cleaning?” She walked back to the circuit box. “It obviously needed it.”

“Then where did he put them?”

“Threw them away? Maybe they weren’t his.” She opened the original box, still empty, and turned it upside down, shaking it.

“I remember them,” Henry said, his voice quiet as he sat down on the stairs at the other end of the basement.

“What?” she asked.

“Nothing.”

“I’m sorry,” Justine said as she sat down next to him.

“Not your fault,” he said. “Thank you for helping.”

“Wasn’t much help.”

A door slammed upstairs, the sound loud in the close space. She jumped, just a little, scooting closer to Henry, her hand resting on his arm.

Footfalls were loud against the wood flooring as someone walked around the house. Henry stood up, pulling Justine with him. He reached up to pull the light cord, plunging them into darkness.

At the top of the stairs, the door stayed closed. Her hand was moist in his, her skin soft and warm.

“Henry?” she whispered, squeezing his fingers.

“Probably my dad.”

“Why are we hiding?” she asked.

The footsteps faded away before another door slammed and then there was silence, save for the constant hum of the air-conditioning.

"I don't know," he said, and started to reach for the light cord.

"Shh," she said, tugging on his hand.

"What?"

"Did you hear that?"

"Hear what?"

In the darkness, she gripped tighter on to his hand. "That."

"I don't hear anything."

"Something's beeping," she said.

Henry turned the light back on but didn't let go of her hand. He blinked in the sudden brightness.

"There it was again."

They stood in silence, still holding hands.

"That?" he asked.

"No," she said, "it hasn't been long enough. It's every thirty seconds."

"You've been counting?"

"Yes." She nodded. "Did you hear it that time?"

"No, you were talking."

Justine reached her free hand up and covered Henry's mouth with her palm. He turned to face her and slid the flashlight into his pocket, bringing his own hand up to cover her mouth. She smiled beneath his fingers as the beep sounded again.

His eyes widened and she took her hand down. "Heard it that time, didn't you?"

Henry nodded and started walking away from the circuit box, into the far corner beneath the staircase. Thirty seconds later, they waited for another beep. After, they took a few more steps on tiptoe, trying to see behind boxes. Another beep.

Henry moved a pile of boxes out of the way until he could see underneath the stairs. An old fire alarm hung off the wall, a faint red light blinking as it beeped once again.

"Well," Justine said, "that was anti-climactic."

"What were you expecting?" He took the battery out of the alarm and tested it on his tongue.

"What are you doing?" she asked.

"Seeing how much power is left."

"With your tongue?"

He held the 9-volt out to her. "Here, just touch the two metal things."

"No thanks," she said. "I trust you."

"It tingles."

"It's electricity. We're already alive—I'm not eating a battery." She shook her head. "Though I could go for a donut."

He pocketed the battery and started picking up the boxes he'd moved.

"Henry?" She was on her hands and knees when he turned to look at her, and all he saw was the way her shorts stretched across the back of very tan, very slim thighs, the shadows playing hide-and-seek with his vision as he watched her sit up. "It's empty."

She passed a small box over to him, the half-ripped-off label still showing part of an address.

"CME-U," he read out loud. "I can't make out the rest, it's missing."

"Does it mean anything to you?" she asked.

He shook his head. "You?"

"Of course, it solves everything," she said. "Do I look like Sherlock Holmes?"

Henry looked her up and down, at the dust stains on her knees, the long tendrils of hair sticking to her neck in the heat, the T-shirt glued to her skin. "I'd have enjoyed the books a lot more," he said.

Justine grabbed his hand and walked back into the maze of boxes, then let go of him with a laugh in order to straighten out the mess.

On the way up the stairs, she turned the light out and reached for his hand again.

In the kitchen, a bag of fast-food burgers sat on the table next to a pile of junk mail. Down the hall at the master bedroom a ray of light bled through the edges of the door, but his father was nowhere to be seen.

"Dinner?" Justine asked, pointing at the table.

"Burgers again," he said with a shrug.

"I'm sorry we didn't find anything."

"I have that box now, not to mention my scrapbook," Henry said. "And a burger."

"And ketchup," she said, picking up one of the packets next to the bag. "I'd still like to see your scrapbook one day."

"I'm free Sunday," he said.

She threw the packet of ketchup at him. "You have a date tomorrow?"

He flinched, his hand a second too slow to stop it from bouncing off his forehead. "Something with my dad. No date."

"Your reflexes kinda suck, you know?"

"I know."

"Sunday?" she asked.

"Anytime."

"Sorry about the ketchup, figured you'd catch it," she said. "Pun intended."

"Still not funny."

She smiled. "Puns are an unappreciated art form."

"For good reason."

"Seems like an awful lot of food for just the two of you," Justine said.

"He's always telling me to eat more."

"My mom's always telling me to eat less."

"It's not all for us. I think maybe he's feeding the homeless or something."

"The homeless?"

"The other night he brought home a lot of food. I think he's leaving it outside for someone."

"Why?"

"After dinner, I found the bag on the back stoop."

"Maybe he's feeding a stray cat?"

"A stray cat that cleans up after itself? The empty wrappers were inside the bag."

"Does he do that every night?"

Henry shrugged, then shook his head. "I don't know. Only saw him do it one time."

"Why didn't you ask him?"

"Honestly?" he asked. "I never see him. Plus, even when he's here, he doesn't actually seem to be here, if that makes sense. The other night, he was talking to someone, but there was no one else in the room."

"See," she said, "this is the creepy house."

He threw the ketchup packet back at her. She caught it mid-flight.

"I can see your backyard from my house," she said.

"So?"

"So, tonight, maybe I'll keep watch on your stoop, check out the neat-freak cat."

As they left the kitchen, Justine slipped her hand back into his but let go before they walked outside. A slight breeze had picked up, salty with the scent of the nearby ocean, but not strong enough to dispel the heavy air or the gnats. Somewhere in the distance a car honked, and a neighbor down the street was mowing. Their arms swung back and forth as they walked next door, their fingers brushing against each other on every swing.

Behind his fall of hair, Henry smiled and then looked at Justine. She smiled back. It was like nothing he could remember.

fourteen

XXX

His father sat at the dining room table when Henry returned to the house, warped plates and plastic silverware next to unwrapped burgers in need of a microwave. A bottle of water beaded in the heat, leaving a ring on the table when Henry picked it up and finished off half of it.

"Got your blood tests back," his father said, laying the paperwork next to his plate and pushing the folder across the table. His skin was pale, tight around his eyes and seemed to sink into his cheeks. He kept licking his chapped lips after every bite of dinner.

Henry glanced at the numbers scrolling down the sheet then pushed them aside. "And?"

"Are you taking your meds?" his father asked. "Some

levels are too low. You need to take them every day, Henry. We've been over this before. Do I need to sit with you every morning and night to make sure you take them?"

"No." Henry took a large bite, staring at his plate as he shook his head. "No."

"It's important you take them. Every day."

"I know." He ripped open a packet of ketchup with his teeth and squeezed it onto the remaining half of the burger. "I'll take them."

"I'm serious, Henry."

"I said, 'I know.'"

They finished the rest of the burgers without talking, his father watching him eat, the scrutiny a heavy weight in the silence.

"Any problems?" his father asked when they were done.

"Problems?"

"Other than the itching? Odd pains?" His father shrugged, looking everywhere but at his son. "Anything?"

I think parts of me are dying, Henry thought, but he just shook his head. "No, nothing, I'm fine."

"Sure?"

"I'm fine," Henry said.

"We'll be leaving after breakfast tomorrow for the hospital," his father said.

"Do I have a choice?"

"You know I don't have the right equipment here. Has to be at work. Won't take too long. In and out, then back home. I promise."

"Fine." Henry pushed his chair back.

"There's more if you want it," his father said, pointing at the plate.

Henry shook his head and walked out of the room.

Henry poured the *Friday PM* pills out after adding *CME-U* to the paper beneath the box. Google had returned too many hits to bother with, from the Cebu Mistumi Employees Union to the Churches Micro Enterprise Unit. None of which remotely helped to explain Henry Franks to himself.

On the desk, each generic pill capsule looked exactly the same, but his father had drilled into him that they were all different, all vital. He had once let Henry help put them together, grinding different tablets into powder and mixing the doses by hand. Pouring precise measurements into each empty capsule. Henry hadn't been able to keep his fingers steady enough to meet his father's exacting expectations and, after that, his assistance was no longer required.

Henry flicked one capsule and watched it crash into the other pills before finally scooping them up and dry-swallowing them one after the other until they were gone.

With his hands on the edge of the keyboard tray beneath his desk, fingers spread out, he looked at the scar around his left wrist. The thin white bracelet was the dividing line between the light and dark hairs on his arm.

He yawned, then pulled a pushpin out of the corkboard over his desk, the sharp tip stained brown. In the dim light of the monitor, the shadows danced around him as he stabbed the tack into his discolored finger and watched the plastic body of the pin wobble back and forth where it stood. A small drop of bright red blood popped up around the fine metal shaft. With his finger, he pushed on the side of the plastic handle. A trail of blood dripped down to the desk.

He pulled the pushpin out and sucked on his finger long enough to stop the bleeding. Switching to his left hand, he pricked each finger in turn, then started on his palm. Small dots of blood spotted his skin. He reached an inch or so above the scar on his left wrist, up his forearm, before making a sound.

"Damn, that one hurt," he said before pulling the final pin out of his arm.

He wiped the blood off with the last tissues in the box on his desk, crumpling them up in a ball and tossing them into the garbage. The place where the pain began on his arm was given a bandage, to mark the spot more than to stem the bleeding. It was higher than he put it the last time he played with the pushpins.

One after the other, he cleaned the tips and pushed the pins back into the wall. A branch skittered across the window, sounding like rats behind the wallboards, and he dropped the last one. Crawling beneath the desk, amid the computer cables and dust, he couldn't find it.

When his phone rang, still in his backpack, Henry cracked his head against the bottom of the desk. He rubbed his scalp, and his fingers came away sticky with fresh blood. He pulled the phone out and flipped it open before pulling the tissues back out of the garbage and holding them to the back of his head.

"Henry?" Justine's voice was almost too soft to hear as she whispered into the phone.

"It's late, isn't it?" He shook his head, trying to clear it. "Sorry, that wasn't what I meant to say."

She laughed. "What did you mean to say?"

"Give me a moment, I'm sure I'll come up with something clever to say eventually ... it's late, isn't it?"

"Yes, Henry, it's late. I was watching your father putting food out on the stoop and figured I'd call."

"Has anyone eaten it?"

"No," she said. "But the food's still there. I'll keep watching for a while."

"You don't need to do that."

"It's not a problem." She started to laugh but cut the sound short. "I've sort of been banished to my room."

"Banished?"

"Exiled? Is that a better term?" she asked. "You know, I came home late today because I was at a friend's house helping him with his *homework*." She stressed the last word and then laughed again.

"I'm sorry," he said.

"Not the end of the world, not yet at least."

"I'm still sorry."

"I can sort of see your window from here," she said.

"You're spying on me?"

"I would be if the trees weren't in the way—I can barely see your yard between leaves and Spanish moss. It's like living in the jungle."

Even over the phone, he could hear the knock on her door.

"Bye," she said, softer than a whisper, and then she was gone.

When he looked out his window, the sharp angle blocked any possible view of the stoop where his father had left the food, and too many trees to count covered Justine's house in shadows too dark to see through. Henry lay down, but when he closed his eyes, he saw the black-and-white pictures of Frank playing in a loop through his memories. He dug his palms into his eyes, trying to banish the photographs, but only managed to start a nosebleed from the movement.

Once more, he fished the tissues out of the garbage. He watched shadows cross the ceiling while squeezing his nose shut to stem the blood.

Frank Franks?

"Henry Franks." He spoke so softly the words were nothing more than a breath of sound, but neither of the names sounded familiar.

Sleep fought him off for a long time, his numb hand resting uselessly on his chest. Just as he thought he might be about to fall asleep, he jerked awake. A quiet hissing sound, high-pitched and frustrated, cut through the hum of the air-conditioning. Henry rolled over, pulling the pillow over his head to drown out the noise.

Elizabeth is there, waiting for me. Her smile, meant for me alone, brings out the sun from behind the low clouds racing across the sky. In my arms, she's light as a feather, floating free and away and I can only watch as the shadows return. Still, she smiles, always smiling, and in return, I smile back. It's the least I can do.

The park is filled with kids, strollers sailing down the riverbanks into the sunset until Elizabeth and I are almost alone. A knife-edge of lightning slices through the clouds, down and down until there is nothing between the energy and the earth but me.

"Daddy, no!" Elizabeth screams as I burn alive.

She is there, waiting for me with a smile. A balloon pops in the distance. Shreds of red latex flutter to the ground in the hazy sunshine. Another. Scraps wrap around my skin.

Pop!

I swallow the balloons, the colors mixing and merging into blackness.

"Daddy, no!"

She is there. I run to her but can't reach her side. She smiles, but not for me. Laughs, at me, but I can't hear a sound. Water bubbles out of my mouth as I try to call her name. Between us, fish swim in and out of view with long tails and each of them smiles at me as they float by. The hook catches the edge of my lips, tugging upwards until I am finally smiling with them.

"Daddy, no!" Elizabeth screams as I drown.

She is nowhere to be found. I search an empty park on a day with no sun and a night with no moon in a sky with no clouds. In the distance, I hear her scream 'Daddy!' but I can't find her. I run so fast I barely touch the ground, until I forget how to run at all and trip over feet I no longer recognize and no longer feel.

Someone's there, helping me up, but it's not my daughter. Too old, and I can't see her face in the shadows and I can't focus on her. She's there, keeping secrets from me and hiding Elizabeth away and I can't stop myself from hating her even as she tries to help me.

"Daddy, no!" Elizabeth screams in the distance as I wrap someone else's fingers around the stranger's throat.

"Daddy, no!" until the woman dies in my arms and the screams are finally silent and I am alone in an empty park on a night with no moon.

NOAA Alert: Tropical Storm Erika Aiming for United States

Miami, FL—August 22, 2009: Tropical Storm Erika is gaining strength and could become a hurricane by tomorrow or Monday afternoon, according to the latest National Hurricane Center reports.

Data from an Air Force Reserve Hurricane Hunter airplane revealed that Erika's wind speed has increased to 70 mph, with gusts even stronger.

The storm system, recently formed off the coast of Africa, is projected to reach landfall in the Caribbean within the week at its present speed.

Local Resident Survives Beating

Brunswick, GA—August 22, 2009: Brunswick Police Department spokesperson Carmella Rawls has confirmed that Elijah Suarez, 27, of Blythe Island, GA, was evacuated by helicopter to Memorial Hospital in Savannah late Friday evening. Suarez, co-owner of SSI Landscaping, was found on the St. Simons Island beach at low tide. Initial reports are that he suffered severe trauma and was unresponsive when emergency personnel arrived at the scene.

"At this time, there is no evidence to suggest that this is related to any previous or ongoing investigations," Rawls said. "We encourage anyone with any information as to Mr. Suarez's activities Friday to contact the Brunswick PD."

Major Daniel Johnson, of the joint task force covering the string of gruesome attacks that have terrorized Glynn County this summer, was unavailable for comment.

Fifteen

XXX

Henry woke with a headache and rubbed his eyes in a vain attempt to relieve the pressure. Distant images from his nightmare danced away from his memory as he looked around his room. The sun lanced through his window, low, hot, and far too bright to face this early in the morning. He sighed, swung his legs off the bed, and stood, bracing himself with his arms against the wall to keep from falling when he stumbled. The scars running down his thighs were puckered, raw, and in spots painful.

The skin on his legs changed tone and consistency from patch to patch, and some sections had long since lost anything more than an odd pins-and-needles sensation. His ankles, circled by a thin white diamond pattern of scars like his left wrist, itched, and he lifted first one foot then the other to rub what remained of the ointment his father made for him into the skin.

He carried the empty tub with him to the kitchen for his father to refill.

"That lasted less than a month, Henry."

"I know."

"Want me to make it stronger this time?"

Henry slouched down in his chair and took furtive bites of his toast. "Yes," he said.

"Itching's worse?"

Henry nodded, not looking up.

"Having nightmares again?" his father asked.

Henry swallowed the last of his breakfast, then pulled his hair down in front of his face.

"Henry?"

"No."

"Sure?"

"I'm fine."

His father walked to the window, taking another look around the backyard. "Almost ready to go?" he asked when he turned around.

"Whenever," Henry said.

"Remember, this isn't an official visit. It'll just be you and me."

"Fine."

"I thought Dr. Saville was working with you about that," his father said with a half-frown on his face.

Henry followed behind as they walked out of the house,

dressed far too warmly for the late August sun. Across the yard, in front of her house, Justine was setting up the sprinkler with her younger brother. Dressed as usual in cut-offs and a bikini top, she waved before jumping into the water.

"Henry?" his father called from the car.

With the door open in his hand, he stood watching her jump in and out of the spray.

"Henry!"

Shaking his head, sending a wave of hair into his eyes, he looked at his father, and then got in the car. They drove off in silence down Sea Island Road toward the Causeway and Brunswick.

Southeast Georgia Regional Medical Center was the largest hospital complex between Jacksonville to the south and Savannah to the north. Constantly under renovation, it boasted a state-of-the-art maternity ward and a turn-of-the-last-century morgue.

They pulled into the staff parking lot and Henry followed his father through a series of tunnels and freight elevators to the sub-basement of the Medical Examiner's offices. One of every three fluorescents was turned off to save money on the weekend, and, of those that remained lit, most were flickering and yellow.

The hallway was made of concrete blocks that had once been painted a calming green, but most had faded to bland. *FORENSICS* was stenciled on the window to their immediate left, and Henry's father had to swipe a card to enter the room.

Despite the ancient setting, the equipment was fairly contemporary and fully functional, a result both of FLETC's overwhelming government presence in the neighborhood and a brief modernization whirlwind when Sea Island had hosted the G8 summit in 2004. Lining the walls were a bank of heavily latched metal doors. In the middle of the room, two autopsy tables, surrounded by light trees, stood empty.

"Lovely office you have," Henry said, trying not to touch anything as he stopped in the door.

"I'm not the Medical Examiner," his father said, pushing a gurney over to Henry. "Here, hop on."

"Excuse me?"

"Just a gurney. The equipment in a morgue is slightly different than most since the subject can't exactly get up on the table by themselves."

"'Subject,' lovely," Henry said as he sat on the bare metal. "Cold, too."

"Next time I'll bring a sheet for you."

"There's gonna be a next time?"

"I'd like to take a look every year or so, make sure everything's all right, even though you say you feel fine."

His father pushed open the doors and wheeled Henry down the hall. The room they entered was dark, and the lights started to flicker to life automatically as the doors opened.

"That's helpful," Henry said as the fluorescent glow finally brightened.

"Ready?" his father asked.

He was about to answer when the door swung back open.

"William?" an older man asked, poking his head into the room. "What are you doing here?"

"Morning, Dr. Sanderson," his father said, after a moment of silence that seemed to last far too long. "My son, Henry, has a school project and I was just showing him around to give him a feel for the hospital. I hope that's not a problem?"

"That's fine," Dr. Sanderson said, waving at Henry. "Your father's a great asset to the team here. Wouldn't know what to do without him."

"Thank you, sir," his father replied.

"Well, I'll leave you to your tour. It's not as gruesome as you'd think from what you see on television, Henry."

Dr. Sanderson turned to leave, his hand on the knob, then looked back over his shoulder. "Make sure I'm set up early Monday morning, William. I have a presentation for the task force on the serial before noon. It'll be doctors only, so you'll need to make yourself scarce."

"Yes, sir."

The doors swung shut behind him as he left and his shoes echoed down the hall long after he was gone.

Henry stared at the floor and ran his fingers through his hair, pulling it down over his face. "I thought—" he said, but he couldn't finish the sentence.

"Henry," his father said. "I can explain." He took a long time to walk around the gurney to sit next to his son.

"I thought you were a doctor," Henry said, still not looking at him.

"I am. Or I guess, I was. It's a long story. After your mother died . . . " He stood up and the gurney rolled a couple feet until it bumped into the wall.

Henry braced himself and watched his father pace the room.

"There was an accident," he said. "She was gone; you were . . . well, you were sleeping."

"I know."

"You remember?"

"No, but you've told me that part before."

His father shook his head, "Yes, I suppose I have. I try to forget some things."

"I try to remember," Henry said, but his father had paced to the far end of the room and didn't seem to hear.

"I chose to stay home and take care of you, Henry. I needed to, for me. Can you understand that?" His father came up to him and took his hand. "I need you to understand. Everything I did was for you. And for her. Always for her."

Henry looked at his hand, unable even to feel his father's touch, and pulled away. Too many questions tumbled end over end in his mind, and it was suddenly far too difficult to breathe. He blinked but his father was still there, towering over him, when he opened his eyes.

What did you do? Henry tried to withdraw even farther from the stranger standing in front of him.

"Henry?"

"What does that mean? 'Everything you did'?"

His father walked back to the far wall, facing the tiling. He straightened his shoulders and turned back around. "I did what I had to do, to save you. To save both of you. Do you understand that?"

Henry nodded, unable to find the strength to say no, and went back to staring at the floor. The cement was slightly concave, leading to drainage pipes. He closed his eyes, trying not to see imaginary traces of blood swirling away down the drain. Somewhere, a far distance away, his father continued talking, but he wasn't sure he still understood the language. It sounded like English but the words were meaningless.

"I stopped practicing, and then you woke up and were well enough to go back to school. I needed a job." He shrugged, then looked away. "And here we are."

"Here we are," Henry repeated after the silence began to stretch once more. Even so, the words were limp and lifeless. He counted to ten, holding his breath the entire time. "Do they know you're a doctor?" he asked.

"No." His father walked back to him, a smile plastered to his face. "It's better this way."

"This is better?"

His father paced back across the room. "No questions. No chitchat with co-workers. I keep to myself and take care of you. To me, that's better."

The silence stretched out, with his father just standing there, staring at him.

"Your mother would be very proud of you, Henry."

Henry shrugged and then looked away. "I wouldn't even recognize her."

Even from the other side of the morgue, he heard his father choke off a sob, but he didn't look up.

"What was her name?" Henry asked, the question whisper-silent.

"Christine," his father said, barely more than a breath of sound. "Her name was Christine."

The name settled in his memories like a long-lost friend, without the alien strangeness that 'Frank' and 'Victor' always carried. Henry closed his eyes, reveling in the comfort of her name.

"Christine Franks," his father whispered.

Henry's eyes flew open. The sense of the long-lost friend was gone, replaced, once again, by a stranger where his mother, for just a moment, had lived within him.

"Christine," Henry said, soft as a whisper. The name, familiar and safe, was a balm and he repeated it. "Christine Franks." He pulled the hair down over his face so his father couldn't see him and mouthed her name again.

Only the first name, he thought, was real.

sixteen

XXX

On Sunday morning, Henry stood in the shower, bitter cold water running over him. He shivered, once, and then stuck his head under the flow. When his teeth started chattering, he stepped back and let the water beat against his legs. Each scar on his thighs trapped the sting, easing the itch, until the skin was numb enough not to hurt. Better that than the phantom itching and spreading death that inhabited so much of the rest of him.

Toweled dry, he felt clean only until rubbing the new ointment his father had left for him into his skin. A fingernail caught a corner of a scar but he couldn't feel the pain. He pulled his jeans on, the sensation of the lotion gluing itself to the denim in the heat even less pleasant than usual.

A pair of scissors rested on his desk and he picked them up, judging where the best place would be to cut in order to turn the pants into shorts. He put the scissors down unused, pressing his palms into his legs in a futile struggle to dull the itch.

He ate cereal alone, sat in his room alone, then, hours later, ate lunch alone. He knocked once on his father's door but there was no response, and when he turned the knob it was locked. Outside, he heard kids playing in the street. A car drove past a few times and a dog barked in the distance. Somewhere else on the island, a church bell pealed.

Henry stared out his window, watching Justine's brother playing with his friends. From the shade of her porch, Justine turned toward his house as though she sensed his presence and he ducked to the side. When he looked back out she was gone. A knock at the door called him away from the window.

Barefoot, she stood on his porch, wearing blue shorts with a big daisy on one leg and a white tank top with a matching flower. She smiled when he opened the door.

"Can I come in?" she asked.

Henry nodded his head and opened the door wider.

"Still too dark in here, you know?" She flipped a switch on the wall but nothing happened. "Well, that was helpful."

"You turned on the outside light."

She flipped it off and tried the next one. There was a yellow flash as the bulb blew out on the wall above them. "Even more helpful." She smiled. "I give up."

"And you wonder why I wear black?"

"You are what you *eat*, not where you live."

"I ate cereal for breakfast and lunch. What does that make me?"

She looked at him as they walked up the stairs. "Wheat?"

"I was thinking corn."

"Where are we going?" she asked.

"I thought you wanted to see the scrapbook." Henry stopped in the short hallway and looked at her. Hot summer sunlight leaked out from the open doors on both sides of them. One room was empty save for a fine coating of dust, and the other was his bedroom. The bathroom door at the end of the hall was closed.

They stood toe to toe with little space to move apart.

"This your room?" she asked as she pointed into the empty one.

"I suppose I could sleep in the closet over there on a hanger."

"That would explain the wardrobe."

"Now see, that was kinda funny."

"I know," she said. "You're learning."

He opened the door to his room but she stayed in the hall.

"Henry," she said with an indrawn breath, her hand coming to rest on his arm as she stopped short in the doorway.

"What?" he asked. "What's wrong?"

"You live here?" She didn't move, only studied the room.

Sunlight cut it in half, leaving shadows dancing along the walls where the branches of the trees outside shifted in the weak breeze. A twin bed took up most of the room. His desk, with the corners of the laminate peeling up, sat near the window with his laptop docked beneath it. Push-pins poked out of the bare white walls but didn't hold up any pictures.

"The only boy's room I've been in is my brother's, and even he has stuff on his walls. Where are the posters? Sports teams? I'd even be okay with swimsuit models." She took a single step into his room and leaned against the wall. "Well, maybe not 'okay,' but, really, anything would have to be better than this, right?"

He shrugged but didn't look at her as he sat on the edge of his bed.

"Any bands you like?" she asked.

He rubbed his palms up and down his thighs, then froze as a blush crept up his cheeks. The scar on his wrist itched despite the numbness spreading over his arms and he tensed his fingers out against the mattress to keep from scratching.

"You don't remember," she said as she sat on the only chair in the room and wheeled it closer to him. She picked up his right hand, rubbing her thumb over the skin. "It's all right, Henry." She stroked his palm until he relaxed and their fingers intertwined.

"It's over there," he said after a number of deep breaths.

"What?"

"The scrapbook."

She pulled him with her as she scooted back to the desk and kept his hand in hers as she flipped open the album.

The first picture showed Henry as a young boy, portrait-posed with his hair combed down and hair-sprayed. A fake smile creased his face and he'd tilted his head as though listening to someone telling him how to sit properly.

"School pic?" she asked.

He nodded, and she turned the page.

A series of portraits, one a year, scrolled across the double page as he aged to early teens.

"Nothing more recent?"

"No," he said. "This last one here was a few years ago, I think."

She turned another page, one after the other. Standing beside her, Henry kept silent.

On its very own page, the picture he'd brought to Dr. Saville's office once upon a time: his parents' smiles as they held him between them.

"Your mom?" she asked, looking from the picture to Henry, then back again.

"Her name's Christine," he said. "I don't remember her, though. Only what my Dad says."

"And?"

Henry was silent for a long time, his eyes restless, moving back and forth between his mother and Justine. He shook his head, then closed his eyes to block both views. "I think he's lying to me," he said.

"About?"

"I don't know." He opened his eyes. She was watching him and the sensation was unlike anything he'd ever known.

"It's just a feeling, when I think about her name, and my dad's."

"What kind of feeling?"

"That the names are wrong." He shrugged. "I don't know how to describe it. When I say her name, it feels right."

"And his doesn't?"

He sighed. "Only her first name feels right."

"And her last name?"

"He's lying," he said and then fell silent. "It's my last name too."

"Does your name feel right?" she asked.

"Henry does."

"And the rest?"

"Is wrong somehow."

"Your mom?"

"He doesn't talk about her much. Just that she died in the accident that took my memory. He's sad a lot, I think."

"Are you?" Justine asked.

"Sad?" He looked at her, the curls of hair escaping down her neck, the steady gaze from honey eyes, and shrugged. "Sometimes, I guess. Isn't everyone?"

She looked away, back to the scrapbook, and turned another page—to the picture of his birthday party with the strangers who should be friends watching him blow out candles in a park he should have recognized.

"Henry," she said, her fingers resting on the picture. "When's your birthday?"

"November 19th. Why?"

Justine looked up at him, squeezing his fingers. "It's not fall."

"So?"

"In this picture. It's doesn't look like autumn. Those trees should have shed their leaves by November, even here in the South. They should at least be a different color."

He stared at the photograph. In the background, behind the picnic table they were gathered around, trees filled with green leaves shaded the park. One of his friends, standing to the side, was in shorts, and all of them were tan.

He'd never noticed anything else before, beyond the faces he couldn't remember.

"Henry?"

With a sigh, he touched the picture, resting his finger on his own face.

"Who am I?" he asked, the words barely more than a breath of air.

His fingers fell limp in her hand and slipped away as he backed up to his bed. He sat, hunched over and rocking back and forth.

"Breathe," he said.

She was on her feet in front of him, her fingers on his arm.

"Henry?" She took his hand and squeezed it between both of hers.

He shuddered at the touch, then looked up at her from behind his hair. A thin trail of blood leaked from his nose, staining his lips a violent shade of red. He smiled at her touch.

"The medicine," he said, barely a whisper, reaching a hand to his nose.

"It's all right, Henry." She wiped his face off with the bed sheet, pressing her palm against his cheek as her fingers ran over his skin. She sank to the floor in front of him and reached out to him. His head rested against her shoulder as she hugged him.

He rocked in her embrace, whispering "Breathe" over and over into her neck.

When he opened his eyes, he watched the pulse in her throat beat in time with his. Sweat glistened on her skin, so very close, and with each deep breath he inhaled her, sweet and feminine and intoxicating. Her fingers ran up and down his back, warm and comforting, and her head rested lightly on his. For a moment, he couldn't even remember his name and didn't care.

He shifted his head a little to the side in order to close the short distance between his lips and her neck and, before he could change his mind, kissed her.

Her hands froze and her breathing stopped. Fingertips flexed against his back, catching his shirt up in her fist as she stretched against him.

He kissed her throat again, right where the blood pulsed beneath her skin.

"Henry," she said, the words spoken into his hair, her lips moving against his scalp.

Outside his window, the sun dipped far enough beneath the tree line to darken the room.

"Walk me home?"

He turned his neck enough to look up at her. "You live next door, you know?"

She smiled, then pushed herself up until she was standing in front of him. He grabbed her hand and stood, then spread his arms and she melted into him.

He tilted his head and looked down at her.

She tilted her head and looked up at him, her honey eyes barely open.

"Justine—" he said.

"Yes."

"I haven't asked anything yet."

"Sorry," she said, and the heat of her breath brushed against his lips. "You talk too much."

Just as they were about to touch, she smiled.

He closed his eyes and kissed her smile.

Justine held his hand as he walked her home. Crickets and frogs, loud in the marshes surrounding the street, accompanied them. The moon had yet to rise and the scattered streetlights fought to penetrate the trees, leaving dappled shadows on the ground. The sun had taken most of the heat with it when it had fallen beneath the horizon.

Justine's mother poked her head out the door and looked down to where her daughter held Henry's hand.

"Almost feels as though we're being watched," Justine said, releasing his hand.

"You must be Henry," her mother said.

"Hello, Mrs. Edwards." He reached out a hand but she didn't move. After too long a time, she shook his offered hand.

"Just friends?" she asked her daughter, then sighed. "Nice to meet you, Henry."

"Good night," Justine said before closing the door, flashing him a quick grin before she disappeared from view with her mother.

Henry stood there, staring at her door after she went inside. He turned around with a smile across his face. The memory of their kiss was still fresh and her lip-gloss was a faint sweetness when he licked his lips. In the distance, heat lightning flashed, casting shadows up and down the street. Thunder rolled and left silence in its wake, the crickets and frogs deathly quiet. The slight breeze that had carried the scent of the Atlantic across the island calmed, leaving the air empty and still. The porch stairs of her house creaked with each step.

A cat screeched down the street and a dog barked in reply. Ozone tickled his nose as another flash of lightning stabbed into the ground somewhere nearby. Thunder hit bass notes deep in the pit of his stomach and he picked up his pace.

A dry branch broke in the shadows as the moon forced its way through the clouds. The back of his neck tingled and he whipped around, thinking Justine had run after him, but there was no one there. Hissing, too close for comfort, floated on the still air and he ran the rest of the way home. He tripped on the porch steps, scrabbling on his hands and knees up the rough wood, scraping his palms, though he didn't feel anything.

Lightning ripped across the sky, the thunder chasing right behind. Still, it felt as though he was being watched. The storm seemed to follow him up the stairs to the door. His heart heaved against his ribs with each pulse, his breathing labored as he slammed the door shut behind him.

He flipped the switch but the dead bulb gave no light in the hallway. Moonlit shadows through the high windows did nothing to dispel the gloom.

The wind picked up with the rain, slamming the branches against the roof. His breathing began to calm as the thunder rattled harmlessly outside.

"Henry?" his father asked from behind him.

He jumped almost high enough to reach the ceiling and his heart took flight again, pounding with the shock. His hand rested on his rib cage, feeling the beating heart racing within.

"Don't," he said. "Don't do that."

"It's just a storm," his father said with a half-hearted laugh. "You're a little too old to be afraid of thunder, don't you think?" He turned and went back down the hall to his room.

Henry took the steps upstairs two at a time. *How old am I?* But like most of the other questions, it remained unasked.

In his room, Henry ripped the photo of the birthday party out of his scrapbook. Green trees, against a high blue sky dotted with white fluffy clouds. The flash caught him just in the act of blowing out the candles on his birthday cake. A tear landed on the picture as he studied it.

The photograph trembled in his grasp, his fingers shaking, tensing around the edges and he dropped it to keep from crushing it into a ball. It fluttered to the ground and landed face-up, staring at him from the floor. Head in his hands, he stared back, unable to close his eyes and too scared to move.

"Breathe."

A pushpin stuck out of the wall in front of him and

he rested his finger on it, trying to feel the hard plastic edge. He let his hand fall, landing on the desk next to the scrapbook, the empty page with his own handwriting on it: *Birthday Party: November 19.*

It wasn't autumn, in the picture still on the floor.

He turned the pages, flipping back to the beginning. He skipped the school portraits, going straight to the first candid shots. He leaned over the book, squinting to see better. He looked at the trees in the background, the grass, flowers, the clothing people were wearing, and the buildings in the corners.

One by one, he looked at them all, unable to even understand what he was looking for. Another birthday picture, an earlier age, the kids in shorts again. He picked up the photo from the floor and compared the kids surrounding him as he blew out candles on the cake. Same kids? Older, at least; similar, maybe.

He didn't know. But again, it wasn't fall.

More pictures, his nose brushing against the archival paper as he studied each photograph. His father had noted his mother where she appeared, a bright smile, dark hair curling around and down her face. Petite, she seemed so small next to his father, the two of them holding hands, smiling, happy.

He turned the page, picture after picture, looking for anything. Another page. Another. His face pressed into the book, he stopped. His mother and father, caught unaware by the flash of the camera. Not quite touching; not quite happy. Something had etched fine lines across his mother's pale skin. That same something had drawn his father's smile down into the beginnings of a frown.

After that, the pictures of them were far less frequent, those of him more staged. On another page, his father, caught in profile, watched his son doing nothing in particular. His father's eyes were hooded, dark, with circles beneath them that were even darker, almost sad. But that's not why Henry stopped.

There were no street names in any picture, no identifying marks of any kind for any reason. No buildings he recognized, no mountains towering in the background. No stray pieces of paper lying around for the camera to capture. He had searched every picture, studied every inch of them, and found nothing except for this one photograph of his father in profile, watching him. No, not sad; there was more pity in the look than that. And beneath the half-frown and the double chin, a faded T-shirt with half an *O* and an *RD*.

ORD?

Henry stared at the letters, blue and yellow against a gray background.

"Breathe."

His computer hummed to life when he pulled the wireless mouse over. From beneath the pillbox he spread out the paper and added the letters to the random list. *Elizabeth. Victor. Frank. Christine. CME-U.* And, now, *ORD.* He hunched over the keyboard as he clicked open Google.

ORD.

Chicago, O'Hare airport; no. Fort Ord; no. He scrolled through the pages then froze, his fingers hovering over the keys.

ORD.

Livets Ord University, affiliated with Oral Roberts and located in Sweden; no. Then, in Google blue: *STANFORD UNIVERSITY.*

"Breathe."

Henry clicked and clicked, exploring the maze of the various Stanford websites, deeper and deeper into the alumni sections, looking for ... what? He didn't know what he was searching for or why, couldn't even figure out if *ORD* was a clue or not. There was no rhyme or reason to his clicking, each link taking him wherever it might. His tears fell on the keys, his breathing spiraling out of control.

Stanford.

"Breathe."

Then, there was no place left to click, every avenue requiring registrations and passwords he didn't have. He shuddered, struggling to draw a breath. His palm slapped against the desktop and his keyboard hopped into the air. The pills, in their plastic coffin, rattled and he dry-swallowed them all at once, coughing as they rubbed against his throat.

He stared at the monitor, resting his finger against the Stanford logo, the red *S* staring back at him. His finger slid down to rest on the desk and then pushed his mouse to put the computer back to sleep.

Staring at the blank monitor, he sat there, unmoving.

He blinked, once, twice, then rested his head down on the keys. With a shove, he pushed himself backward, the wheels squeaking over the wooden floor. The chair bounced against the wall and Henry bounced with it.

He crawled into bed fully dressed, pulled the covers up over his head despite the heat, and tried to convince himself that pretending to sleep was as good as the real thing. Anything not to dream again.

NOAA Alert: Erika Upgraded to Hurricane; Cuba on Alert

Miami, FL—August 24, 2009: The National Hurricane Center is reporting that Tropical Storm Erika has now been upgraded to a Hurricane as wind speeds have topped 100 mph. After the storm made a northward turn in the direction of North America, the government of Venezuela stopped broadcasting Hurricane Alerts for the coast. The projected path has been updated to indicate landfall in Cuba and the Gulf Coast by the end of the week.

A Tropical Storm alert has also been issued for the Netherlands Antilles islands of Aruba, Bonaire, and Curacao for the imminent arrival of Tropical Storm Danny, with sustained maximum winds of 65 mph.

eighteen

XXX

Henry woke on the floor, tangled in blankets. Memories of a nightmare disappeared as he struggled to cling to his dream. An image of a touch, the feel of a glance, but nothing made sense as he kicked the sheets off. While he brushed his teeth, however, all he thought of was a kiss.

The sun was already hard at work burning the dew off the grass as he walked to the bus stop. He stood at the edge of the sidewalk, balancing on the curb. Along the road, a handful of other kids congregated apart from him and all he could do was watch as they laughed at a joke he couldn't hear.

Justine walked along the street, kicking a pile of grounded moss as she wandered from side to side, keeping in the shade of the trees that lined Harrison Pointe. As she approached she grasped her backpack, holding it in front of her like a shield. She stared at the ground between them, studying his shoes. Her mumbled "Good morning" was barely audible.

"Justine?" he said, his hands deep in his pockets as she took a step back from him.

She looked over her shoulder, to where her mother stood on their front porch, and, without looking at Henry, took another step away. Before she'd taken a third, she stopped.

"Damn," she said as the bus pulled up.

Kids piled up the stairs, jostling to reach the same seats they always sat in. The clatter of latched windows being forced down echoed through the bus. The benches squeaked.

Henry sat, slid over next to the window, and watched as Justine worked her way up the aisle. Staring at her feet, she bumped into the girl in front of her and stumbled backward. With a blush, she sat down in the seat in front of Henry and stared straight ahead.

He leaned toward her as the bus pulled away from the curb. "Justine?"

She looked at him over her shoulder, her hair curling down around her face, then lowered her eyes and turned back around.

"You all right?" he asked, resting his hands on the back of her seat.

Without a sound, she nodded.

Henry sat back, his fingers resting for a moment longer on the vinyl before falling to his lap. She cast a quick glance back toward him before turning away again. Conversations grew and died around them, replaced by laughter and the quiet sounds of kids fanning themselves with whatever was handy.

"What words end in 'ORD'?" Henry asked, bending his head forward to speak to her neck, not really sure how to be the one to actually initiate a conversation with her. Her skin glistened in the heat, a stray strand of hair sticking to her back.

Her head came up but she didn't turn around.

"In one of the old pictures of me and my dad, he's wearing a shirt that says 'ORD.' I'm thinking Stanford."

"Oxford," she said, her voice soft. Then she turned around, her eyes lighting up with the words. "There's Oxford, too, in England. Probably lots of others. You think that's where he went to school?"

Henry smiled back at her and shrugged. "You okay?" he asked.

Her smile wavered, but she stayed facing him with her arms on the back of the seat. "I told you my mother wouldn't be happy."

"Bad?"

"She's a little old-fashioned."

"Old-fashioned?"

"She's forbidden me to date you."

"We're dating?" Henry asked.

She laughed, then closed her eyes and stilled her smile.

"No. Just … damn, she saw us holding hands." Justine barely said the words out loud and a fine blush ran up her cheeks. "I don't know, Henry. What are we doing?"

The bus pulled into the high school and the noise grew in volume. Henry leaned closer, resting his forehead on the green plastic of her chair. When he finally looked at her, he was smiling.

"Will you sit with me on the way home?" he asked.

Justine held her backpack in front of her as they made their way off the bus. "Yes," she said before walking into school next to him.

In the hallway in between classes, her pink toenail polish passed by. When he looked up to wave she was looking back, but there wasn't time for much more than that in the crowded hall. Before the bus pulled away to take them home, however, she squeezed in beside him. Her fingers rested in her lap before he reached over and traced her thumb. She wrapped her hand over his, holding it against her thigh, and they drove the entire way home just looking at their hands, joined between them, in silence.

They walked together from the bus stop, but she'd let go of his hand before they got off the bus and they didn't touch as they approached Henry's house. Next door, her mother popped her head out.

"Later?" he asked.

"I have a plan," she said, before turning away and running home.

In his house, Henry trudged up the stairs to his room and tossed his backpack in the corner. His computer booted up with a touch and he sank into his desk chair, studying the pattern of pushpins in the wall.

There was a knock at the front door. Another, louder, more insistent, and he scrambled down the stairs.

"It's hot out here!" Justine said, her fist preparing to knock again. "Can I come in to help with your homework?"

Henry shut the door behind them. "We have homework?"

"Had to think of something, and she probably sees right through me, but ... " She smiled. "It worked, didn't it?"

Henry shook his head, trying to clear it. "This was your plan?"

"I'm here, how about we leave it at that?" She reached for his hand as they walked up the stairs. "So, Stanford?"

He sat at his desk, Justine standing next to him, and brought up the alumni website. "No access, so I gave up."

"Call them," she said, pointing at the contact information taking up the bottom quarter of the screen.

He laughed, a short bark of a sound. "No."

"Why not? It's either that or hack their site, and I can't do that, can you?"

"No," he said. His shoulders slumped and he looked up at her.

"Let's call; they're three hours behind us."

"And say what?"

She smiled then shook her head. "Hi, my name is Henry Franks?"

"Not a chance," he said with a laugh. "You can call, if you want to."

"Okay," she said.

Henry stood up, the desk chair rolling back. He looked at her bright eyes and big smile as she stared back at him.

"I was kidding," he said.

"Phone?" she asked.

He fished his cell out of his backpack and they sat on the floor with it as Justine dialed.

"What are you going to say?" he asked.

She shrugged as the line connected and she clicked the speaker on.

"Stanford Alumni, may I help you?"

Justine closed the phone, cutting the connection, and turned bright red. "Oh, damn, I'm sorry," she said, laughing.

"What was that?" he asked.

"Sorry," she said, still red, still laughing. "I'll be serious. Seriously, I will be."

She sat up straighter, a frown forced onto her face.

"Serious?" he asked.

"Serious."

Justine flipped the phone back open and clicked redial. She took a deep breath as the ringing came through the speaker.

"Stanford Alumni, may I help you?"

"I'm sorry," she said, her southern drawl just a bit more pronounced than usual. "We must have gotten disconnected."

"No problem, happens all the time."

"I'm hoping you can help me," Justine said. "My future father-in-law went to Stanford, and he was telling me the other day how much he regrets losing his yearbooks in a fire a while ago."

"Oh, I'm so sorry to hear that."

"Well, I was thinking what a wonderful gift it would be if I could replace them for him."

"I'm sure he'd love that. Do you know when he attended Stanford?"

Justine looked up at Henry, his fingers pressed over his mouth to keep from laughing and his skin a couple different shades of pink. He shook his head and shrugged.

"No, I'm sorry," Justine said. "I just came up with this idea, so I'm not really sure."

"Let me look him up and see what I can find for you. What's his name?"

Henry grabbed a notebook out of his backpack and scrawled a name across it.

"William Franks," she read. "Dr. William Franks."

"A doctor? Maybe he went to our med school."

"I'm not sure, sorry."

"I'll check for you. Can you hold?"

"Absolutely," Justine said as music floated softly out of the speaker.

"I can't believe you!" Henry whispered.

"You have a better idea?" She smiled at him, resting her fingers on his arm. "I can't hack a computer but I definitely know how to talk."

"Are you there?" the woman asked.

"Yes, ma'am," Justine said.

"I have 27 'William Franks' at Stanford, but that's stretching back to well over one hundred years ago. I think we can narrow that down a little. How old do you think he is?"

Justine looked at Henry, who scribbled a number down, then added a question mark after it.

"45ish?" Justine said. "Maybe. Somewhere in that neighborhood."

"Well, undergrad might have been mid-eighties, med school late eighties. Let me check." The clacking of keys came through the speaker as Henry wrote down the dates.

"Three for the decade of the eighties. None of them in the med school. One of them was a late-eighties undergrad so that's probably wrong. Leaves a William Franks graduating in 1983 and 1985. Does that help?"

Justine jumped up, the phone rocking in her hand. "Yes, yes, of course. How would I be able to replace the yearbook, though?"

"The Alumni department stores leftovers offsite so I'd have to check on the year, but do you really want to order both?"

"Oh," Justine said as she collapsed into the desk chair.

She rolled over next to Henry and rested her fingers on his shoulder. "Any suggestions?"

"Can you hold a moment?"

"Yes, of course," she said as music piped into the room. "We found him!"

"Maybe," Henry said from the floor.

"Spoilsport." She stuck out her tongue at him.

"Then what?"

"'Then what' what?" Justine asked.

"We see what he looked like; what do we do with the information?"

"Oh," she said as the music stopped.

"Are you there?" the phone asked.

"Yes, ma'am."

"We do have both years in storage. Do you have an email address? I can scan their photos in and you can tell me which year you'll need. Will that work?"

Justine rattled off her email and slowly closed the phone, a bright smile on her face. She stood up, shaking her fingers. "I can't believe I did that! And my mom says no good can come from being talkative. Ha!"

She spun around, then jumped, pumping her arms in the air like a prizefighter after a knockout.

She stopped, pulled Henry up beside her and forced the frown back on her face. "Serious enough?" she asked.

"Perfect."

"Seriously?"

"Very much so," he said.

"I'm gonna go check my email. I'll forward what they send me."

"Thanks."

"Walk me home?" She smiled, taking his hand and leading him down the stairs.

Justine spread her fingers as they stepped outside, her palm sliding away from his, and looked over at her house.

"Sorry," she said, not even looking at Henry.

"It's all right, I guess."

"Friends?" she asked, walking so close that she kept brushing her shoulder against him.

"You'd be the only one." He squinted against the sun dipping toward the horizon.

"Friends," she said.

"I'd like that," Henry said.

"Me too."

His computer was waiting for him when he sat back down at his desk after dinner. He explored the Stanford alumni sites, both official and not, but there was nothing of interest to find. Not that there was a Step Two if Step One provided any answers. Knowing where his father went to school didn't solve his problem, or resurrect his memory or his mother.

From his backpack his cell phone started ringing and he flipped it open. Justine's voice sounded thin and distant, muffled.

"Henry? I just got an email from Stanford."

He sank into his chair, staring at the logo on his monitor. "And?"

"It's not him."

His shoulders slumped and he closed his eyes.

"Henry?" she asked.

"I'm here, sorry," he said. "Not him?"

"One's African-American and the other one is deceased, died in 1991. Not him."

"Thanks for trying," he said after a long pause that threatened not to end.

"I'm sorry," she said. "I thought … I mean, I … "

"It's okay, Justine. It's not your fault."

"There's Oxford," she said. "And probably others, and maybe hundreds of high schools, Ridgeford and Washford and Stepford and Fordford, I don't know, there has to be, don't you think?"

"Going to call all of them?" he asked, releasing his breath in a long slow stream, almost a whistle.

"I'm sorry, Henry."

"Me too." He looked up, moved the cursor to the X in the top right-hand corner of the screen, and closed the Stanford window.

"You all right?"

He shrugged even though she couldn't see it. "Not really sure what I was going to do with the information anyway."

She laughed. "You could always just ask him, couldn't you?"

"We don't—" His voice cracked on the word. "It's not that easy."

Henry turned off the light, crawling on top of the sheets with the phone on speaker lying on his chest.

"I'm sorry," she said again.

"Not your fault. I'm used to it."

"Still sorry."

"Thanks," he said, then let the silence play out. If he listened carefully, he imagined he could hear her breathing. The breeze blew a stray branch against his window, a light tap, followed by the whisper of her breath that seemed so close it was almost as though Justine was in the room with him.

"Justine?" he said.

Silence, save for the hiss and the tap.

"Hello?"

He picked the phone up in the darkness just as it started to ring.

"Sorry," Justine said. "Got disconnected. Must have lost the signal there for a minute. Did I miss anything?"

Still, the hissing and the tapping, so close.

"No," he said. "Nothing. Just the wind."

"Night, Henry."

"Good night, Justine."

"Sweet dreams," she said before the phone went dead.

Victim of Beating Wakes

Savannah, GA—August 24, 2009: Brunswick Police Department spokesperson Carmella Rawls has confirmed that Elijah Suarez, 27, has recovered sufficiently from his injuries to provide information to authorities.

According to Major Daniel Johnson of FLETC, a growing profile of the random attacks that have occurred in the Golden Isles this summer has been enhanced by the active participation of Suarez.

"[His] back took a beating," said a spokesperson for Memorial Hospital in Savannah who requested anonymity because they were not authorized to speak for the hospital. "Multiple contusions and breaks. He's lucky to be alive."

Patrols on Jekyll Island have, at the request of the Jekyll Island Authority, been supplemented by National Parks Service personnel on loan from Skidaway Island, Crooked River, and other park locations throughout Georgia. In addition, the Georgia Bureau of Investigations has provided logistical support to the task force.

"We continue to support the efforts of all law enforcement here in Glynn County in order to resolve this unfortunate situation as quickly as possible," said Mayor Monroe.

Brunswick Man Identifies Assailant; Police Say No Apparent Connection to Previous Murders

Brunswick, GA—August 25, 2009: Unofficial sources have confirmed that Elijah Suarez, 27, of Blythe Island has provided a detailed description of his attacker to the police.

"There wasn't a lot of moonlight that night," said one police officer on condition of anonymity due to the sensitive nature of the information. "Suarez got one look at her and was able to assist a sketch artist in producing the first real break in this case."

Stepped-up patrols have blanketed Glynn County with the sketch of a woman who appears to be in her late 40's or early 50's with cloth bandages covering her hair. A Caucasian female with partially healed scratches on her face, wearing ratty clothes; she is estimated to weigh about 130 pounds.

According to Suarez, she didn't say a word as she clubbed him with her fists and a length of pipe, and police have been advised that she appears to be highly dangerous but unarmed.

"She spit at me, no tongue or something; couldn't understand a word she said," Suarez said through an intermediary from his room at Memorial Hospital.

"At this time, despite the injuries sustained by Mr. Suarez, we are still unable to tie this particular attack to any of the previous incidents that have happened here in Glynn County over the past few months," said Major Johnson. "We are dedicating all of our resources into locating the alleged suspect and resolving this matter."

Margaret Saville, PhD
St. Simons Island, Glynn County, GA
Tuesday, August 25, 2009
Patient: Henry Franks
(DOB: November 19, 1992)

"How's school?" Dr. Saville asked, her pen tapping against the pad.

Henry looked out the window trying to follow the path to its end. Behind a scruffy palm tree, a brief glimpse of ocean. Heat warped the air, distorting his vision.

"Henry?"

"Studying Shakespeare," he said without looking at her.

"Poems or plays?"

"'To sleep, perchance to dream.'"

"*Hamlet*. Is that it?"

He closed his eyes and turned toward her, "No," he said. "Nothing."

"Justine?"

He blinked, once, twice.

"You're smiling, Henry, and blushing. Justine?"

"I had another dream," he said, running his fingers through his hair.

The pen stopped tapping. "Justine?" she asked again.

Against the fabric of the seat, his fingers flexed,

stretching out and back, before he pushed himself off the couch. Two steps brought him across the room and the doctor shrank back between the high arms of her chair as his shadow fell over her, blocking the light from the window.

"Henry, please sit back down and let's talk."

"I had a dream."

"About Justine?"

"No," he said, staring at the white path in the garden leading nowhere.

"Have you been practicing your breathing exercises?"

He shrugged. "I breathe. Does that count?"

"Will you be standing there long, Henry?"

He rested his forehead on the glass, absorbing the heat through the window. His hands rested on the smooth surface, fingers pressing down. He counted to ten in silence, then shrugged again.

"Where does the path go?"

"The path?" she asked, rising to stand beside him.

He pointed, his discolored finger tracing the route against the glass. "It goes nowhere."

"Does that bother you?"

With a sigh, he turned to face her. She held the legal pad between them, the pen clutched in her fingers.

"I don't know," he said. "I can't remember if I like gardens."

"Process."

"I know," he said, then walked away and collapsed back onto the couch. "I don't think I want to remember any more."

"Why?" she asked, leaning back against the windowsill.

He closed his eyes and the silence stretched out with his breathing.

"Henry?"

"I kissed her." He smiled.

"Justine?"

"Yes."

"And?"

"She kissed me back."

"That's good, isn't it?" Dr. Saville asked.

Henry looked at her, his smile fading away, and then his head dropped down to his chest and he hid behind his hair again.

"I don't want to die," he said.

She looked up at him, her breath catching on a cough. "Excuse me?"

"I had a dream."

"What happened?"

"I couldn't find her. Elizabeth, she was gone and I couldn't find her." He wiped his eyes then rubbed his nose on his sleeve. "Then, I remembered the last dream, where I killed her and I realized I'd never see her again. She's dead."

"You're not Victor." Dr. Saville crossed the room and knelt down next to him.

"She's never coming back. In my dream, I had nothing more to live for."

"Henry?"

"I killed my daughter."

"Just a dream," she said.

"I killed her mother."

"Henry, look at me." Dr. Saville took his hands in hers, her fingers ice cold. "Henry."

"I don't want to die. I kept saying that but no one would listen."

"Who wouldn't listen?"

"Elizabeth. She couldn't hear me. No one heard me." He pulled away from her, rubbing his fists into his eyes. A single drop of blood snaked down from his nose, leaving a red trail around his lips. Dr. Saville grabbed a tissue off the desk and handed it to him. "No one ever hears me."

"It's all right, Henry."

"I killed myself," he said.

"In your dream?"

"After killing Elizabeth." He shuddered and closed his eyes. He took a single breath and held it long past a count of ten.

"Breathe, Henry."

He gasped, sucking in air. Stars danced in the corners of his vision as he hyperventilated and collapsed back in the chair.

"Deep breaths, Henry."

"I don't want to die." He tilted his head to the side, looking up at her with a smile highlighted in blood. "I miss Elizabeth."

"Just a dream, Henry," she said.

"Justine is helping me remember."

"You said you didn't want to."

"Would it change anything?"

"You tell me."

He looked at her and then shook his head. "I remember dying."

"That was a dream."

"I guess I don't want to remember, but I'm afraid that someday I'm going to."

"That's a healthy step," she said.

He brushed his hair back off his face. A trail of tears ran down his cheeks, mixing with the blood.

"What if I don't like me?" he asked.

"What if you do?"

"That's not an answer."

"Did you expect one?"

"What happens next?" he asked as the alarm beeped.

"We find out where the path leads."

The salt of the Atlantic lingered on the hot early morning breeze when Henry opened the door. As he walked up the street, he looked over his shoulder toward Justine's house and slowed his pace when her door opened. He stopped completely when she appeared.

In a white sundress with a yellow belt, Justine flowed down the street, moving from one patch of shade to another. Her hair caught the wind, swirling around her like a cloak, hiding everything but her smile. When she stopped in front of him, she brought the shade with her.

"You," he said before turning around to look for the school bus.

"Yes?" she said.

"Morning."

"You too." She walked up beside him, facing the oncoming bus. "Did you know that high schools in England are called secondary schools? Didn't help much, though, to be honest."

"Help?" he said as they found their seat and sat down.

"Well," she said, twisting around to face him, her leg caught up beneath her. "He doesn't have a British accent, right?"

"Who?"

"Your father. I was bored. You were asleep, remember?"

He shook his head, then smiled. "Start over again."

"Your dad, not British, not in secondary school in England. I checked a few Oxford-related school listings, didn't find many William Franks in their class annuals, very helpful, no pictures though. But, since the years didn't really work, I gave up. With me now?"

"Yes," he said. "I think."

"It's like looking for a needle in a haystack."

"I know."

"No, it's worse," Justine said. "It's like looking for one particular needle named William among all the needles in all the haystacks. Have you figured out what you're going to do if we find out where he went to school?"

Henry shook his head, a half-frown on his face.

"You still could ask him."

"He's never even home anymore. No one to ask."

"Where is he?" she asked.

"I don't know. Work?" He shrugged. "I don't think he sleeps much."

"You all right?"

He looked at her. A loose curl caught the wind from the open windows, warm honey eyes welcoming him along with her smile. "I think so."

"Ever look for those pictures again?"

"Everywhere but in his bedroom."

"Why not?" she asked.

"It's always locked, even when he's not home. So I don't even bother anymore."

"Locked?"

Henry shrugged.

The metallic shriek of the brakes as they turned into the high school carried through the bus. With the motion, Justine slid against his shoulder.

"Any plans this weekend?" he asked.

She looked up at him, her hair falling between them. "Any time in particular? Like, say, Friday night?"

"Friday night would be good," he said with a smile.

"As long as the hurricane turns north, no plans at all."

"Didn't they tell us in school that they always turn?"

"Pretty much. It's the elbow effect," she said, bending her arm to show him. "Hurricanes tend to prefer Florida or South Carolina. Georgia's protected."

"Would you want to see a movie or something?"

"Like a date?" She smiled, running her fingers through her hair to tie it up in a ponytail.

"Like a date."

"Yes," she said. "Although of course it'll have to be approved by my parents. But for the record, my answer is yes."

They were almost inside the school, walking next to each other, when she reached for his hand.

twenty

XXX

After school, Justine left Henry at the metal gate that never closed and ran into her house where her mother had watched them walk from the bus stop.

Henry went inside and hadn't gone more than halfway up the stairs when there was a knock at the door.

"Mom said 'maybe' for Friday, which is better than 'no,' right?" Justine asked as he opened the door for her. "Looks like movie dates don't have to wait til senior year after all. But still, we'd have to have company—that all right? Unless we have to evacuate for Erika."

"Company?"

"Well, the technical term would be 'chaperone.'" She smiled.

"That's all right," he said with a matching smile.

The photographs from the scrapbook were laid out on the bed in as close to chronological order as Henry could make them. The picture with the half-seen T-shirt worn by his father leaned against the monitor on the desk, next to a pushpin sticking out of the wood. Justine sat in the chair as Henry moved some photos over to sit down. She picked up the picture, staring at the shirt.

"Not Stanford, not Oxford."

"I've Googled everything I can think of," he said, running fingers through his hair as he leaned back against the wall. "Know how many states have cities with 'ford' in them? And most of them have high schools. Now add all the other words ending with 'ORD' that you came up with."

"Giving up?"

"Still not sure why I'm even looking," he said, then pushed the pictures to the ground. "So I learn where he went to college. Doesn't help me remember my own life. Just his."

Justine wheeled the chair over, bumping up against the bed, and rested her hands on his shoulders, pulling him toward her. "You shouldn't give up, Henry."

"Why not?"

"Well, first off, researching this with me has been fun, right?"

He ran his thumbs over her fingers then rested his forehead against hers. "Right," he said. "And second?"

"Well," she said, leaning back to look at him. "I'll have to get back to you on that. Still, it's fun even if we're looking for something we'll never find and, really, don't even have to. Besides, it'll give us something to talk about on our date."

"You always have something to talk about, Justine."

She blew him a kiss and pushed off, rolling back across the floor. On the desk, the pushpin poked her arm. "Ow," she said. "Why is this even here?"

Henry stood up next to her and pulled the pin out of the wood. He rolled it between his fingers before resting the pointed tip against his left palm, eyes locked on Justine as he pushed it in.

A small red dot of blood welled around the metal shaft, and he smiled.

Her mouth shot open as she reached for him. "Henry!" she said, but he backed away from her, his hair falling in front of his eyes as he pulled the pin out.

"A few months ago, only this finger." He pointed his discolored index finger at her. "Didn't feel anything, but the numbness has been spreading recently."

"Spreading?" she asked.

He poked the pin into his forearm, almost up to his elbow, then again, higher, leaving a trail of red dots up his arm. An inch below his biceps, he stopped.

"That one hurt," he said with a small frown, pulling it out. "Last week it was below my elbow."

"Why?" she asked.

He shrugged, then stuck the pushpin back in the wall. He slid the pillbox out from behind the monitor and flipped the lids, one at a time, until the entire box was open. "Lots of pills, since the accident. My dad keeps trying different combinations, different dosages. Some give me nightmares. Or make my nose bleed. I'm not sure if the numbness is a side effect or a symptom. Can't really Google me."

"I know," she said.

"You know?"

She handed him some tissues from her purse and helped him wipe the spots of blood off of his skin. When he was done, she traced his scar with her finger. "I Googled you. Didn't find anything. Thought there might be something about the accident, but I didn't even know where to look."

"I'm ungoogleable."

"Is that a word now?" She smiled.

"Absolutely."

"Really? What happens if I Google 'ungoogleable'?" She typed as she spoke. "Well, I guess I shouldn't be surprised at almost 8,000 hits, should I?"

He shook his head. "Not even a little."

"See, that's why we're looking for your father's school."

"Why?"

"Maybe that will help us Google you," she said. "That's reason number two."

"Is that the best you could come up with?" he asked.

"It's short notice; I'm sure I'll come up with something better eventually." She laughed. "I always do, don't I?"

"Usually," he said, trying not to laugh along with her.

She bent over the pillbox, studying the medicine piled in each compartment. "Nightmares?" she asked.

"About my daughter."

"Elizabeth?"

Henry closed the pillbox and pushed it to the side. The small piece of paper caught on the corner and he spread it open.

Justine picked it up and read off the names. "Victor. Elizabeth. Christine. Frank. ORD. CME-U, I remember that one. That wasn't much help to Google either. Is this your research list?"

"What there is of it."

"Who's Victor?"

"Elizabeth's father."

"Ask her for last names," Justine said, handing the piece of paper back to him.

"Who?" Henry folded it up and put it under the pills again.

"Elizabeth," she said. "In your dream, ask her."

"I'm not sure..." Henry said, and then fell silent. "They're not that type of dream, I guess. Does that make sense?"

"They're your dreams, Henry," she said. "Can't hurt to try."

"They're not."

"Not what?"

"My dreams," he said. "Though I once asked her my name. That's how I learned about Victor."

She looked up at him and then reached out for his hand, running her fingers up to where the pin had left its mark on his skin. "Ask her for me?"

He nodded.

"And no more pushpins."

Henry pulled them out of the wall, one by one, and lined them up on the desk. Their metal tips were stained as they bumped against each other. When he'd pulled them all down, he rolled them into her hands and watched as she dumped them in the trash with the wadded-up tissues.

"Better?" he asked.

She smiled. "Have you told your father?"

"About?" he asked.

"The numbness?"

He shook his head. "No," he said. "I tried a couple of times, but no."

Justine clasped his hand again, pulling him toward her. "Can I ask for another favor?"

He nodded.

"Tell him?"

Henry smiled but didn't answer.

"Promise?"

"Yes," he said. "Anything else?"

The sun peeked out from a cloud and for a moment the room lightened. She tilted her head to the side, her tongue resting on her lower lip. "You could kiss me again."

The clouds closed back up and a sudden breeze brushed

the branches against the window. Beneath the scrape of leaves and wood on the glass, the wind hissed and, if he listened hard enough, it seemed to moan, rattling the shutters.

Henry ran his fingers over her cheek, tracing the curve of her skin from where her earlobe met her jaw, down her neck, and back to the soft skin hidden beneath her hair. His thumb rested behind her ear and he could feel her breath against his lips.

"God," she said, soft and warm against his skin, "I hope you can feel this." She pulled him just that much closer, her arms clutched around his shoulders, and kissed him.

The wind shook the door, almost as though it was testing the knob, trying to get inside.

NOAA Alert: Erika Category Three; Eastern Seaboard Alerts: Florida to South Carolina

Miami, FL—August 27, 2009: The National Hurricane Center has reported that Hurricane Erika has reached Category Three on the Saffir-Simpson Hurricane Scale with maximum sustained winds of 125 mph as it continues on its path toward the eastern seaboard of the United States. Hurricane alerts have now been issued by the National Hurricane Center from Key West, Florida north to Myrtle Beach, South Carolina.

Hurricane force winds extend outward to thirty miles from the center and tropical storm force winds extend outward over 125 miles.

twenty one

XXX

When Henry turned the corner into the kitchen the next morning his father was already at the table, elbows on the edge and his face deep within the steam of his coffee.

"Dad?"

William waved the fingers of one hand but kept staring into his mug. "Morning," he said, though the word was slurred and soft. With an obvious effort, he shook his head and looked up. "Morning," he said again.

Henry stood at the refrigerator door, looking back at his father. Thin hair streaked with gray lay flat against his skull, the ridges of the bone almost poking out of the dry pale skin. The circles under his eyes had grown and his smile was nothing more than a brief twitch of his lips.

"What?" he asked.

"Nothing," Henry said, then turned back to the refrigerator.

"Just tired," his father said.

"I didn't say anything."

"How are you?"

Henry sat down with his breakfast, not looking at his father across the table. "Fine."

"Fine? Is that what this is?"

"What?" Henry asked.

"Nothing," his father said, drinking down his coffee and pushing the mug away. "Are you taking your meds?"

"Yes."

"I hope you realize how important they are."

"I know," he said. "You keep telling me."

"I'm serious, Henry."

"I said, I know. I'm taking them."

"And the ointment? Do you need more?"

"No. Not yet."

"Your tests," his father said. "They looked good, really."

"Okay."

"Anything new?"

Henry looked up. The wind hissed against the window and his father flinched. Henry shook his head. "No."

His father stood and walked across the kitchen, then stopped in the doorway. "Henry?"

"Yeah?"

"Dr. Saville," he said, and then looked away. "Is she helping?"

"Helping?"

"Do you remember anything?" he asked, the words forced through gritted teeth. "About before?"

Henry pushed his chair back without answering, dropped the bowl and spoon in the sink, then walked to the front door with his father following behind.

"Henry?"

"What is there to remember?" he asked, opening the door to let the bright morning sun shine in.

"Your mother," William said. His hand reached out, lingering in the air close to Henry's shoulder but not touching. "Anything."

Henry turned around and his father lowered his arm. "No."

The wind picked up, branches banging on the windows almost hard enough to break the glass. His father flinched, slamming the door shut, bracing it with his back. Eyes wide, he pushed Henry down toward the kitchen.

"What?" Henry asked, trying to slide out of his father's grasp. "Stop!"

"Quiet," William whispered. "Come on."

"Why?" He dug his heels in, sliding over the wooden floor as his father pushed and pulled at him, dragging him away from the front door.

A loose shutter beat against the siding, the deep bass thud of wood striking wood drowning out the cries of the wind. From somewhere far away, a horn honked and then, faintly, there was a knocking at the door.

"No!" his father screamed, squeezing Henry's arm to keep him from answering the door.

Henry shook off his father's hands and ran to the window. A branch poked the glass as he looked out.

"Justine," he said, and slid open the bolt to unlock the door.

Behind him, his father turned the corner and disappeared into his room as Henry stepped outside.

"I heard screaming. You all right?" Justine asked.

He shook the hair out of his eyes and looked at her. "My dad was freaking out about something. Weird morning," he said as they walked toward the bus stop.

"Did you talk to him?"

"No." He shrugged. "He looks like he hasn't slept in weeks. He's never home, and when he is he asks random questions. Just weird."

"It's the summer for weird." They sat down on the bus and she squeezed his fingers. "Can you feel that?"

"Not really," he said. "But it's okay."

She traced her finger up his arm, over the scars. "Tell me when," she said as she went higher and higher.

When she was beneath the sleeve of his T-shirt his breath caught. "When."

Justine looked around, then leaned down. She lifted the edge of his sleeve and kissed his shoulder.

"When," he said, again, softer.

"It's higher," she said.

"I know."

"I'm sorry."

"Don't be. It's not your fault I'm falling apart."

"Is that what you're calling it?" she asked.

"It's better than saying that parts of me are dying." He turned to look out the window as the bus rumbled over the causeway.

"Henry," she said, the word little more than a whisper.

He turned to face her, but when he went to touch her she pulled away.

"Talk to your dad," she said. "You promised."

"I know."

She wiped her eyes and then reached for his hand, the hint of a smile just touching her eyes.

"Any news on Erika?" he asked as the bus reached the end of the bridge.

"Probably South Carolina, my dad says. Should turn north soon; they always do."

"What if it doesn't?"

She shrugged. "Might hit Savannah, maybe? They were kind of hit back when I was younger, like five or so. My mom was telling me they evacuated for Floyd."

"Evacuated?"

"She lived in Savannah, then. Nothing here in Brunswick, though."

"You sound disappointed," he said as the school bus pulled up to the curb.

"Nothing ever happens in Brunswick," she said. "Well, except this summer." She ran the tips of her fingers over the scar circling his index finger. "Did you have a dream last night, Henry?"

He shook his head. "I usually don't dream if I take my pills."

"Going to take them tonight?"

"I don't know."

"Maybe you'll learn something new?"

"You're not going to let this go, are you?" He laughed.

Justine shook her head. "How about I call in the middle of the night? If it's a nightmare, it might wake you up."

"That's the silliest idea ever," he said.

"Is that a no?"

"No."

Justine smiled. "I was going to call even if you said no."

"I figured."

They walked off the bus and into the school, not hand in hand but close enough to touch.

"Frankenstein!" the voice came from behind as Bobby walked in between them, splitting Justine away from Henry.

"What's your problem?" she asked, trying to walk around Bobby, but he kept moving to block the path. A small crowd of kids was gathering in the hallway around them, trying to look like they weren't paying attention.

"No problem. Just saying hi to Frankenstein here," Bobby said.

"Actually," Henry said to Justine before she could respond, "that *is* better than Scarface, and you did ask him if that was the best he could do."

"Well, to be technical, the monster didn't have a name. Frankenstein was the doctor," Justine said before turning back to Bobby. "You might want to work on that some more. Maybe a six out of ten?" she asked, looking at Henry.

"I think the East German judge was a little harsh," he said. "Probably at least a seven."

A burst of laughter came from one of the students behind Bobby as he opened his mouth to speak.

"Maybe I could glue on some bolts," Henry said, pulling down the collar of his shirt to show off the scar circling his neck. "It could be part of my look."

"I've told you before, you don't really have a look," Justine said. "More of a unique personal style."

"I'll take that," he said, turning back to Bobby, who pushed past him and continued down the hall.

Justine moved in closer, sliding her hand down his arm until their fingers merged. "Does that mean I don't get to be Igor?" she asked with a laugh. "I want to be Igor."

"Now see," Henry said, "*that* was funny."

Margaret Saville, PhD
St. Simons Island, Glynn County, GA
Thursday, August 27, 2009
Patient: Henry Franks
(DOB: November 19, 1992)

A handful of clouds, gray and hinting of rain, rode the wind across the sky. Henry watched them from between the slats of the blinds. Behind him, the ticking of the clock and the tapping from Dr. Saville's pen counted out the time.

"How are you doing, Henry?" she asked.

He turned around to face her, leaning against the windowsill. "Was a good day. Better than 'fine,' at least."

"Something happen?"

He sank into the couch, his finger idly tracing the scar on his wrist.

"Henry?"

"There's a hurricane coming," he said.

"Want to talk about it?"

"No, not really." He smiled. "Justine says it'll turn north. They always do."

"Are you ready if it doesn't turn? Medicine and everything?"

"Dad said he'd make more. He stocked up on milk and bread and candles. It'll be an adventure."

"You were speaking of Justine?"

"I was?" He ran his fingers through his hair, pulling it down to hide behind.

"Henry."

"We're dating, I guess. I think she's my girlfriend."

"Is that a good thing?"

"So far," he said. "She says it's been a weird summer."

"Has it?" Dr. Saville asked.

Henry lay his head on the back of the couch, staring at the ceiling. "What would you like me to compare it to?"

"You were awake last summer, and bored, you told me."

"No hurricanes last summer." He looked at her, unblinking. "Or serial murders."

The pen tapped against the paper as a cloud crossed the sun and the first drops of rain splattered against the window.

"Or girlfriends," she said, then placed her free hand over the pen, muting the tapping.

"Weird summer," he said as a clap of thunder rattled the pane of glass and lightning sliced through the sky.

"Have you been having any nightmares, Henry?"

"No, not since she died."

"Elizabeth?"

Henry closed his eyes and draped his elbow across his face. "Her mother. I killed her."

"You're not Victor, remember?"

"Are you sure?" he asked, then turned away from her.

"How old was Elizabeth?"

He shrugged where he curled up in the corner of the couch. "Young. I don't know, exactly."

"Did she talk to you?"

"Yes."

"So, old enough to talk?"

He nodded.

"How old are you, Henry?" she asked.

"Sixteen."

"So, say Elizabeth was five. Does that sound reasonable? Do you think you had a child when you were eleven?"

He looked up at her, blinking rapidly in the light. "No." There was a spark of relief and something approaching hope in his voice. "I'm not Victor."

"No," she said. "You're not Victor."

"I miss her."

"Just a dream."

"Still," he said.

"It's all right, Henry. Not having any more nightmares is progress." She stood as the alarm went off. "Tuesday?"

"Unless there's a hurricane." He smiled. "You ready?"

"Candles, bread, water. All set."

"It'll turn," he said, stopping at the door to look back at her.

Out the window, through the slats of the blinds, the white path leading nowhere was flooding in the rain.

twenty two

Henry looked out at the parking lot outside of Dr. Saville's office. The rain was coming down in sheets and he could barely see his father's car waiting for him at the end of a row. He pulled his shirt over his head and ran out the door, jumping over puddles and bouncing off a car as he slipped on the wet pavement. His T-shirt was soaked before he'd taken more than a dozen steps, and flashes of lightning threw shadows around him. At the door to his father's car, he pulled the handle but nothing happened. He pounded on the window for his father to unlock the door.

Long moments passed with Henry hitting the glass with the heel of his palm, not even feeling the impact. He ducked down, squinting to see inside. A flash of lightning illuminated his father, slumped over the wheel. Henry ran around the car, sliding through a puddle and ramming his shoulder into the bumper of the minivan next to him. His ear rang from hitting the light fixture above it, but he didn't feel any pain.

He stood up, unsteady, shaking and soaking wet, and made his way around the car. He rubbed his ear, still ringing, and came away with his fingers dripping blood. At his father's door, Henry banged on the window, leaving a trail of blood to wash away in the rain.

When there was no response, Henry started kicking the door, denting the metal before his father finally stirred, tilting his head to look up at him. Henry wiped the rain away and stuck his face up close to the window.

"Unlock the door!" Thunder drowned out the words and the sound of his father pressing the unlock button.

Inside the car, Henry dripped on the seats and tried to wipe the rest of the blood off his face. "Have a nice nap?" he asked.

"Sorry," his father said as he started the car. "Lost track of time. You're bleeding, what happened?"

"I slipped."

"You okay?"

Henry shifted away from his father, turning to the window to study the trails the rain was making down the glass. "Fine."

"I said I was sorry, Henry."

"I said 'fine.'"

A ray of sun broke through the clouds as the rain slowed

on the brief drive home. In the driveway, William stayed in the car as Henry got out.

"You coming in?" Henry asked.

His father shook his head. "No, too much to do."

"Whatever," he said, then slammed the door.

Behind him, William rolled the window down. "Henry!"

He turned around, standing in what remained of the rain. "What?"

"I'm sorry."

"Will you be home at all?"

His father shrugged, rolled the window up, and pulled out of the driveway, leaving Henry standing in the middle of the front lawn. He looked at Justine's house, waved even though he didn't see anyone, and walked to the front door.

One by one, he searched through wet denim pockets for his keys, hoping they weren't with his cell phone in his backpack still in his father's car. He tried the knob but held little expectation that it would work, and wasn't surprised when it didn't.

"Just fine," he said, resting his head on the door. "Crap."

The wind chilled his wet clothes as he climbed up on the porch railing to reach the spare key in the gutter. His shoulder popped as he reached up over his head and his ear was still ringing from the car he'd run into. With a grimace, he walked his fingers back and forth in the gutter until he finally pulled out the spare keys.

Up and to the right, he unlocked the door, then threw the key-chain back into the gutter.

William parked down the street from the house, watching as the wind blew the branches through the rain. His stomach grumbled but there was little desire to eat, to drive somewhere and buy something. He sighed and unrolled the window, letting the water splash his face as he looked into the marsh.

With a shudder, he pushed the door open and ran between the houses. Back to where the trees were lost in shadow, his feet slipping in the mud. Still, he kept moving, chasing the wind to find where the hissing began. But there was never anything there when he arrived. A branch broke, the echo right behind him. He spun around, her name on his lips, but he was all alone. Always alone.

Walking through the trees, he wiped the rain away from his face with muddy hands and left streaks of dirt behind. Another branch broke and he took off running toward the sound. The rain blinded him and he stumbled, twisting his ankle, but he kept going, chasing the sound.

Behind a tree, he saw someone walking through the woods, long hair whipping around in the wind. William slipped again, sliding into a tree. The figure turned around at the noise. The person screamed, voice lost in the storm, and then ran.

Showered and warm, Henry pushed the case of pills from one end of his desk to the other, counting out the days until he ran out. Enough for now; nothing else mattered.

His father had come home long enough for fast food burgers before he left the house again. Henry rescued his backpack and his cell phone—no missed calls—and then went back to staring at his pills. Taking them would let him sleep without dreaming, no nightmares and no dead daughter calling out his name. He thought of Justine and put the medicine back, closing the pillbox.

A branch scurried against the glass, trying to claw its way in, and the wind moaned beneath his window as he lay down on his bed, cell phone beside him.

"Victor." She calls my name, her red-gloved hands resting protectively on her belly, swollen in pregnancy.

I can't see her eyes, hidden behind layers of red cloth, wrapped around her from head to toe. There are fingers grasping mine, pulling the bandages away from me, and she calls my name. So soft, gentle, these names she calls me.

"Victor."

And I answer, the words whisper-quiet as I struggle against the bonds holding me down, dripping red cloth from manacles and leather restraints where they keep her hidden away from me, tearing my daughter from my arms.

"Victor."

But I stopped listening to her long before she told me she was pregnant; even before she died or I killed her or either of us were born. It was there, in the silence that was the loudest noise of all, the single gunshot, between our daughter's eyes behind those red-gloved hands, resting so protectively against her belly, swollen with pregnancy like an over-ripe melon spoiling in the sun.

That was the final curse. That sun, too hot, even in the rain, creating steam and heat and I can't remember if I ever saw snow.

"Victor."

But I remember my name.

I remember my name.

I remember.

"Victor."

I loaded the stolen gun or stole the loaded gun, I forget. Doesn't matter now, anyway; it's just a dream, Elizabeth, go back to sleep. Hush, little one, just a dream, Daddy's here; it's just a dream. I love you.

I remember that, at least.

Go back to sleep, sweetheart, Daddy will protect you from the monsters under the bed, the witches in the closet, the ghosts in the attic.

"Victor!"

Even when she screams my name it's so soft, gentle in the evening breeze, quiet as a whisper shattering with the crack of the bullet against the bone. Who, I ask her as she unwinds the red bandages so I can see her face before she dies, will protect Elizabeth now?

Me. I answer myself. I'll protect you, Elizabeth. I promise.

And she's here.

So close I can reach out for her, touch her, hold my daughter in my arms and rock her to sleep.

But when I try, my hands pass right through her. A ghost. A mist. Insubstantial.

I'll protect you, Elizabeth.

I promise.

And she's here.

"Elizabeth?" Her name forces its way out of my mouth, as though someone else is speaking through me and I can't stop the words. Can't not speak.

She looks at me, her eyes dark as a night without stars.

"What's your last name?" I ask, but that isn't my question, not what I was going to say. Where did those words come from?

I'll protect you, Elizabeth, I wanted to say. I promise. But then different words sounded, in a different voice.

"Ask Victor," she says.

"I'm Victor."

"No."

"No?"

"Can I go now?"

"What's your last name?"

I'll protect you, Elizabeth, but the words go unspoken.

"I don't remember, Daddy," she says. "I'm sorry."

I promise.

The voice is silent for a long time before finally speaking words that mean nothing to me.

"What's Mommy's name?"

Red bandages cover her, dripping like blood from wounds

I can't see. They twist around her body, covering her mouth, and when her answer comes the voice is mine.

"Alexandra."

And then she's gone and my voice is my own again, but there's no one left alive to hear me.

twenty three

XXX

The ringtone on Henry's cell phone was drowned out by the wind but the vibrations against his fingers woke him from the dream, lingering images less important than the name echoing in his memory.

"Hello?" he said, and then again, louder, "Hello."

"It's me." Justine's voice was quiet as Henry checked the time on the phone.

"I noticed. It's past midnight."

"There's someone in your backyard, eating the food," she said.

Henry scrambled out of bed, sliding on bare feet across the floor. He bent the miniblinds away from the window but couldn't see anything. "What?"

"Looks like a bag lady. She's scratching at the side of your house like she's trying to get in. Can't you hear her?"

"No," he said. "Only the wind."

"It's her," Justine said. "There's no wind. I can't see all that well with the trees in the way and the lighting isn't much help. She seems really hungry."

"Why is my dad feeding a bag lady?"

"Go downstairs and ask her," she said.

"I'm not dressed and half asleep," Henry said. "It's the middle of the night."

"And there's a bag lady eating dinner in your backyard. You don't find that interesting?"

"Interesting, yes," he said. "Worth getting dressed and—"

"She's leaving!" Justine interrupted him. "Get dressed fast, we'll follow her."

"No," he said, but he was speaking to nothing, the call disconnected. With a sigh, Henry pulled on a pair of jeans, shoved his phone in a pocket, and put on his sneakers. He hugged the wall on the way down the stairs, avoiding the squeaky areas in the middle, looking toward his father's room. The light was on, bleeding out from the bottom.

Henry stepped outside. He closed the door softly behind him and was about to turn around when Justine spoke, sending his heart rate through the roof.

"Took you long enough," she said, the words whisper-quiet.

"Did I mention it's the middle of the night?"

"Come on," Justine grabbed his arm. "She went this way."

They walked between their houses, hand in hand. A faint path wound beneath the oak trees and they had to duck under the long tails of Spanish moss hanging from the branches. From somewhere in the marsh a frog croaked, the sound loud in the night. With each step they heard the squelch of their own feet breaking out of the muddy ground. The breeze was just enough to send the moss waving back and forth, distorting their vision and sending shadows to and fro as they squinted to see what might, or might not, be a footprint or two.

Though sounds seemed to carry oddly, this close to the marsh, the distant hissing was a constant companion. The deeper they went into the dark, the louder it seemed to grow. Their hands grew damp in the humid air and Justine let go in order to wipe her palms on her pants.

"This was a good idea, no?" he asked, struggling to keep his voice level.

"I think," Justine said, taking his hand again, "that I've had better ones."

"I didn't take my pills tonight," he said.

"And?"

"Alexandra." Henry said the name out loud for the first time. "Her mother's name was Alexandra."

"Does that help?" she asked.

"I don't know. This crazy person I know woke me up so that we could take a romantic moonlit stroll in the middle of the marsh."

"There's no moon," Justine said. "And it would be more romantic if it weren't so creepy. All that's missing are violins."

"You're not helping," Henry said. "And I have no idea where we are."

Justine stopped and turned around, pointing back the way they'd come. "I think we live that way. Maybe."

"Maybe?"

"Only one way to find out." Justine wiped her hands once again, then ducked underneath a low-hanging branch, Spanish moss grasping after her as she headed down what might once have been a path.

"Wait up," Henry said, rushing to catch up to her. He picked a piece of moss out of her hair and then took her hand.

The smell of ozone was heavy in the air, the first hints of another storm coming to the island. The mud soaked through their shoes, weighing them down, and the moon cast pale intermittent shadows as it played hide and seek with the clouds. The hissing was everywhere as they stepped around a giant oak tree. Moonlight broke through the clouds, casting odd shadows everywhere.

Henry pulled Justine to a stop before she could step out of the darkness and into the small clearing.

In the pale light, the bodies might only have been sleeping, except for the insects and the blood surrounding them.

Justine screamed and took a step back, the sound echoing through the marsh.

Henry pulled her toward him and she shivered in his arms, her teeth chattering despite the heat.

"I think they're dead," she said, her voice barely more than a whisper.

A cloud passed in front of the moon and the clearing fell into darkness.

"Me too." Henry took a deep breath, counted to ten, and exhaled. "Breathe," he said.

And she did.

Together, they took a breath. And another, until she stopped shivering in his arms.

"Better?" Henry backed away so he could see her face. Tears had left faint trails on her cheeks and she wiped them away as he looked.

"A little, I think."

Behind them, a branch broke. Henry spun around, slipping in the mud, and fell down next to one of the bodies.

"Justine," he said, his voice rough and strained, "we need to get help."

She started to walk over to help him up but stopped after only a couple of steps, her fingers covering her mouth. Most of the color had drained from her skin, leaving her pale and maybe a little green around the edges.

"Call 911," Henry said, vainly trying to wipe the mud off his pants.

"We don't even know where we are."

"They'll find us, just call."

After hanging up the phone, Justine cried softly and when he reached a hand out to her, she melted into him.

"We should call your parents," he said.

She looked up at him and frowned as she took her phone back out. "Mom?" she said, turning away from him.

Even from where he was standing, he could hear her mother's voice as Justine talked with her. Henry took his own phone out and dialed his father, but there was no answer.

"She's going to wait for the police," Justine said when she was done. Tears mixed with the mud on her face. "She's not very happy with me at all."

Henry spread his arms and she stepped forward again. He hugged her, stroking her back, and was still holding her when they heard the sirens cutting through the night.

"What are we going to tell them?" she asked.

"You'll think of something more believable than the truth."

"I've still no idea what the truth is," she said.

"Welcome to my life."

Flashlights crisscrossed the marsh, sending shadows around Henry and Justine. They called out to the police, to help them find the clearing. Uniformed officers surrounded them, barking questions over each other as someone else began to rope off the area around the bodies. Bright lights came on, running on generators they'd brought with them.

Justine's mother ran toward them, calling her name. She wrapped Justine in a hug.

"Henry." Mrs. Edwards looked at him. There was little welcome in her voice. "I knocked on your door until your father answered. He's on his way."

"Thank you," Henry said.

"What were you doing out here?" she asked, turning to her daughter.

"I'd like to know the answer to that as well, if you don't mind." One of the people broke away from the two bodies on the ground. He was dressed in blue jeans and a FLETC T-shirt, a badge around his neck. "Major Dan Johnson, U.S. Army." He stretched a hand out to them, his grip quick and firm. "And you are?"

"Justine Edwards, my daughter," Mrs. Edwards said. "I'm Louise Edwards. This is Henry Franks."

"And I'm his father, William," Henry's dad said as he entered the clearing. "What's going on?"

"Justine? Henry?" Major Johnson asked, looking back and forth between the two of them.

Justine looked at Henry, then pushed herself away from where her mother still had her wrapped in a hug. "We got a little lost," she said, the words hesitant and shaky.

"What were you even doing out here?" her mother asked.

Justine looked at Henry and then turned to face her mother as Major Johnson spoke again.

"It's a little late for a walk," he said.

"I thought I heard something," she said. "In the backyard."

"So you called Henry and followed?" her mother asked. "In the middle of the night?

"I didn't feel safe walking in the marsh alone," she said

with a shrug. "I felt safer with him." Justine looked up at her mother but seemed unable to meet her eyes.

"I'm afraid we're going to need the clothes you're wearing, both of you," Major Johnson said, pointing at Henry and Justine. "Routine, you understand, but just in case. When I have more questions, and I will, I know where to find you. In the meantime, the next time you hear a strange noise in the middle of the night, I'd suggest calling the police."

Officers escorted them home through the marsh, flashlights cutting the night into sections as they walked in silence, Henry and his dad a few feet behind Justine and her mom. As they came into sight of their houses, the hissing resumed, so loud it seemed to be throbbing beneath their feet.

"Your father leaves in the morning for Savannah, Justine," her mother said.

"I know."

"No, you don't know, young lady. He probably won't be able to get back to sleep tonight. Because of the two of you."

"I'm sorry."

"Henry," her mother called back to him. The four of them stopped between their houses. "I'm afraid Justine is going to need a rain check on that so-called date tomorrow night. Well, I guess that would be tonight now, no?"

"Date?" Henry's father asked.

"I'd like to say it was a pleasure finally meeting you, Mr. Franks," Louise said. "I've stopped by a couple of times but no one ever seems to be home." She smiled but there was no warmth in it. "Maybe we'll try this again later?"

"I think that would be best, yes," William said.

"Let's go, Justine," her mother said as she started walking toward the house. "Time to give your clothes to the police." She threw her hands in the air and shook her head. "Words I never thought I'd say. Good night."

"Good night," Henry said, before following his father into his own house.

Henry sat at his desk, his fingers running over the holes in the wall where the pushpins used to be. His monitor was dark and the only light was from the moon shining through the clouds. He spun around at the knock and the door opened.

"It's been a long night," his father said, taking a step into the room.

Henry shrugged and turned to look out the window, trying to think of what to say to the man standing in his room. What questions to ask. Instead, he closed his eyes without speaking. His breath caught and he fought even to remember how to count to ten. The numbers tripped over themselves, leading nowhere as one very simple question kept repeating inside his head: *What's your name?*

But he didn't say a word.

"Henry?" his father called to him, his voice soft and hesitant.

He opened his eyes but didn't turn around, watching the wind push the branches against the side of the house, reaching for him.

"She seems nice," his father said, but the words just hung there, ignored.

Henry took a deep breath and counted to ten, the numbers falling in to place like long-lost friends.

"What were you thinking?" his father asked. "It's not safe out there, don't you know that?"

He pushed off against the window and let the chair spin around so he was facing his father. The sudden motion made his father take a step back, and they stared at each other in the moonlight. Henry's nose was bleeding and blood dripped off his chin one drop at a time.

"No place is safe," he said, and only then wiped his face.

The wind picked up, pushing the clouds back in front of the moon. What little light there had been disappeared. A branch crashed against the house. Henry turned on his monitor and a soft glow filled the room. When he looked up, his father was shaking, his fingers trembling. His eyes were wide open and far too red. Thin strands of dirty hair were pasted to his skin with sweat.

The corners of his mouth twitched, as if he was trying to smile, and then he walked out of the room. His fingers shook on the doorknob as he left. Right before the door closed completely, he stuck his head back into the room.

Henry looked at his father, trying to remember the man in front of him, but the memories were gone, as though they'd never existed.

"I love you," his father said, his voice breaking on the words before he let the door swing closed.

Moonlight flooded the room as the clouds broke apart. Branches clawed the house. Henry sat there, counting until he couldn't count any higher, his breathing ragged and harsh as blood dripped to the floor. He looked at the space where his father had been, studying the shadows, looking for answers but there were none to be found.

"Who are you?" he whispered as the moon disappeared again, the words nothing more than a sigh.

NOAA Alert: Hurricane Watch: Florida to South Carolina

Miami, FL—August 28, 2009, 6:47 AM: FOR EMERGENCY RELEASE:

The National Hurricane Center has issued a Hurricane Watch for the following counties along the Florida, Georgia, and South Carolina coastlines:

- St. Johns, Duval, and Nassau counties, Florida
- Camden, Glynn, McIntosh, Liberty, Bryan, and Chatham counties, Georgia
- Beaufort, Colleton, and Charleston counties, South Carolina

Landfall is estimated late tonight on the east coast of the United States.

Two More Victims Discovered on SSI

Brunswick, GA—August 28, 2009: The discovery of two more victims in the marshes on Saint Simons Island late Thursday evening has increased the pressure on the Glynn County Task Force to solve the string of murders that has plagued the Golden Isles this summer.

Florence Josephs, 54, of Sterling and her youngest son, Wayne, 23, were found by local residents Henry Franks and Justine Edwards.

"Due to the continued danger that this situation presents to citizens and to visitors to Glynn County, I have asked Major Johnson of FLETC to seek additional help from both the Georgia Bureau of Investigation and the FBI," said Mayor Monroe.

In response, Major Johnson has requested further involvement, as well as an additional force of FLETC personnel to augment the local and park police already involved with the manhunt for the person police believe has been responsible for these murders.

Initial reports indicated that Florence Josephs died of blunt force trauma and her son died from asphyxiation. The wounds, according to Sam Alli, the first officer on the scene, appear to be consistent with the other murders.

"Again, we ask everyone in Glynn County to remain vigilant and cautious until this situation is resolved," said District Attorney Staci Carr.

In related news, police are seeking any leads regarding the graffiti spray-painted on the pier in Saint Simons Village. The vandalism, which read "If she doesn't get us, Erika will," has been cleaned up at County expense.

Continued on next page

"At this time, it is vital that everyone remain calm and remember to stay safe," Mayor Monroe said. "I have been in direct contact with the National Hurricane Center and as of now, landfall is still difficult to determine. Evacuation plans are being updated and school buses will be available for those needing emergency transportation. As always, we appreciate the support and understanding of the citizens of Glynn County and the visitors to the Golden Isles."

twenty four

XXX

Low dark-gray clouds settled to the horizon and the wind came in fits and starts, tainted with salt and ozone, pushing warm moist air through the open school bus windows.

"I can't believe we're getting a hurricane and it's on a weekend," Justine said. Her head rested back on the seat with her raincoat bunched up as a pillow. "We're not going to miss any school for this."

"What if they evacuate?" Henry asked. "Maybe we'll be out all next week?"

"Wouldn't an evacuation have started already? We didn't even get out of school early. My mom wanted me to stay home today. That's why I missed the bus this morning."

"She still mad?"

"Mad? No." Justine tried to smile but, for the first time Henry could remember, the attempt failed halfway through. "But she's as close as I think she's ever been. What about your dad?"

"I think he knows why we were out in the marsh," Henry said.

"He said something?"

He shrugged and dropped his hand onto her arm, sliding down her skin until their fingers merged. "He came up to talk but didn't really say much. Then he left."

"He went out?"

Henry nodded. "I don't think he's been home since."

"My dad never got back to sleep. He left really early to get to Savannah. Now, *he* was mad at me."

"I'm sorry."

"Not your fault," she said. "I've always wanted to be the one who says that." She smiled. It almost succeeded.

"So tonight's really not going to happen?" he asked.

"After last night, there won't be any movies for a while, chaperoned or not," she said with a shrug. "And my parents are pretty much blowing off Erika, though my dad did nail up some boards this morning before he left."

"Am I allowed to say I'm sorry again?"

"No."

"Then neither are you," he said.

She sat up and turned to face him. "I still think my mom's beginning to like you. She's said yes to us once, you know."

"I know."

"That was a big deal, her saying yes."

"Yes," Henry said.

She squeezed his hands and smiled. "I went to the guidance counselor today."

"About the—" He looked around, then lowered his voice. "You know, from last night?"

She frowned but it was short-lived. "No, I wanted to ask about colleges. Ones that might end in 'ORD.'"

"And?" he asked.

"She said Oxford first; it's where she went."

"Our guidance counselor went to Oxford?"

"Not *that* Oxford. She went to Emory, in Atlanta. But they have a two-year college called Oxford. She went there before transferring to the university."

Drops of rain blew through the windows and Justine drew her jacket over their heads.

"You don't think . . . ?" he said, hidden with her beneath the raincoat.

"Can't hurt to check."

He leaned back and looked at her. "Thanks."

"Haven't found anything yet."

"I know." He ran his finger down her cheek, then held her face between his palms. "Thanks for still trying."

She closed her eyes, resting her head down on his hands for a moment. Then she smiled. "Did you ever search for Alexandra?" she asked, opening her eyes to look at him.

"No. I completely forgot by the time we got home and then, with everything else, it just slipped my mind."

She pulled the coat closed around them and kissed

him as the bus pulled up to their stop. "Then what are we waiting for?"

Together, they ran down the street, keeping under the trees to avoid the rain. In front of his house, she stopped and looked next door. "Crap, I have to go home."

"I understand," he said.

"I'll call." She gave his arm a quick squeeze and then ran home alone.

NOAA Alert: Hurricane Watch: Florida and Georgia

Miami, FL—August 28, 2009, 3:16 PM: FOR EMERGENCY RELEASE:

The National Hurricane Center has updated its Hurricane Warning for the following counties along the Florida and Georgia coastlines:

- Duval and Nassau counties, Florida
- Camden, Glynn, McIntosh, and Liberty counties, Georgia

Landfall is estimated late tonight on the east coast of the United States.

twenty-five

XXX

The house was empty and almost chilly, the air-conditioner working through the humidity outside. Henry took the stairs two at a time, letting his backpack fall to the floor as he turned his computer on. He sat down for just a moment before pushing the chair away and pacing the confines of his room, keeping his eye on the monitor slowly coming to life. On his third circuit, he pulled the chair behind him, spinning it around.

From his backpack, he grabbed notebook paper and a pen, centered them next to his keyboard with the page of names from beneath the pillbox and sat down.

A knock, and then, "Anyone home?" Justine called from downstairs.

"Up here," he yelled back.

She came in, dropped a large duffel bag on the floor, and sat down.

"Going somewhere?" he asked.

"My mom left a note saying she had to go into Brunswick to pick my brother up from school and then run down to St. Mary's to get my grandparents. They don't drive. She asked your dad if he could take me along if there's an evacuation." She shrugged. "Apparently he said yes."

"Well," Henry said, "except for the fact that my dad's not home at the moment, that sounds good to me."

"Where is he?"

"Unlike your mom, my dad isn't the note-leaving type," he said. "The last note he left me apologized for the note before."

"I'm sure there's a really good story behind that," she said.

"Not really."

"Well, in that case, what are we looking up first?" she asked.

"Google just gave me almost eighteen million hits on Victor, Alexandra, and Elizabeth. I need a last name, or maybe a city at least.

"So, Oxford it is," Justine said.

On the screen, the Oxford alumni page loaded and he turned the monitor toward the bed so she could see.

"Do they have class listings?"

"Even better," he said, clicking his way through the site. "It looks as though they have class pictures."

"Individually?"

"No, split up by residential areas."

"Do I want to know how many dorms?" she asked.

"Only four are listed." He shrugged. "But that's today. There might have been fewer back in the eighties. I don't know."

He continued clicking through the alumni section until the small black-and-white thumbnails were displayed.

"They're not labeled all that well, are they?" Justine moved next to him, leaning on the desk to get closer to the screen.

"No."

"The last numbers have to be the year, don't you think? Maybe we can narrow it down a little."

One by one, they opened pictures and read through the names at the bottom.

"Would be easier if these weren't scanned in. The resolution isn't that great," she said, her fingernail running along the monitor.

After dozens of pictures, Henry stretched against the seat, his bones cracking with the motion. Outside, the rain continued, the clouds so dark it might have already been night.

"Hungry?"

"And thirsty," she said. "But just open the next one; we can eat later." She pushed the mouse herself as he turned back to the monitor.

"We're up to 1983," he said. "Are we even close to running out of pictures?"

What seemed like hundreds of grainy photographs later, Justine rested her finger on the names at the bottom of a picture, the quality so poor that faces were blurred together.

"Henry," she said, pointing toward the faint type where *Williams, Frank* was listed.

Beside her, he was silent as his discolored finger rested on the monitor next to hers.

"Is that a typo?" he asked.

"I don't know." Her voice was softer than before, her breath hot against his skin. "Your dad's William Franks, right?"

"So he says," Henry whispered. "I can't see the face. It's too blurry."

"Google it."

Henry opened a new window and carefully typed the name into the search field. "Williams comma Frank," he said, the words barely spoken.

Google returned almost thirty million hits.

"Try 'doctor'?" Justine said.

Eighteen million.

"Try it without the comma?"

Dr. Frank Williams, he typed.

Over eight million hits.

"Put it in quotations."

He re-typed and hit enter.

NOAA Alert: Hurricane Warning: Florida and Georgia

Miami, FL—August 28, 2009, 6:57 PM: FOR EMERGENCY RELEASE:

The National Hurricane Center has issued a Hurricane Warning for the following counties along the Florida and Georgia coastlines:

- Nassau County, Florida
- Camden and Glynn counties, Georgia

Landfall is estimated late tonight on the east coast of the United States.

twenty six

Rain poured down in sheets. The windshield wipers put up a good fight but did little good. A line of cars snaked across the bridge off Saint Simons, and a single car drove slowly through the storm over the causeway onto the island. William hunched over the wheel, wiping his sleeve over the inside of the window to clear away the condensation. He followed the yellow reflectors and the streetlights, barely visible through the storm.

When he rolled down the window to try to improve visibility, the rain whipped into the car, pelting his skin. On the side of the road puddles grew large enough to have their own current, flowing across the street and cascading upwards like a fountain as he drove through them. Wind clawed at the car and whenever he sped up in frustration the car hydroplaned and he gripped tighter to the steering wheel.

The links scrolled down the screen, page after page as Henry kept hitting *Next*. Dr. Frank Williams, Chief Medical Examiner, Jefferson County, Alabama. Trials and evidence and citations in newspaper articles; countless tiny black-and-white pictures of his father.

"Henry?" Justine said, her hand resting on his shoulder. "CME, remember? Chief Medical Examiner. And look, University of Alabama, Birmingham. CME-U."

He breathed. In. Out. Again. He breathed and remembered nothing.

"Henry?" she said. "Talk to me."

He clicked on an item at random, scrolling through the windows. Link after link, Google traced his father's history in Birmingham until the articles stopped.

"Is that you?" Justine asked, her finger resting on the screen.

"Dr. Frank Williams," he read from the caption beneath her hand, "and his son Henry, 13, at a 10K walk/fundraiser for cancer research."

"You're bald," Justine said.

With sunken eyes, a pale smooth hairless skull, and a defiant smile, thirteen-year-old Henry stared at the camera, holding tight to his father's hand.

"Cancer?" he said, the word as quiet as a sigh.

"Google 'Henry Williams,'" Justine said, her grip on his shoulder tightening. "In Birmingham."

The links made for a far shorter list than that for his father.

Outside, rain patterned the windows. Dark clouds raced across the sky and the wind pushed against the house, banging the shutters that hadn't been nailed down properly. A crash of thunder shook the room and the lightning slicing open the sky sent crazy shadows behind them.

Henry followed the links to short notices in the *Birmingham News* about thirteen-year-old Henry Williams: Relapsed Acute Myelogenous Leukemia and stem-cell transplants and countless sessions of chemotherapy as they walked the annual 10K. The Chief Medical Examiner and his dying son. Raising money so that, just maybe, others would live.

From around the island, evacuation sirens cut through the storm as thunder rolled across the sky.

Justine squeezed down on his shoulder, her fingernails digging into his skin through his shirt, but he didn't feel the pain. "Henry," she said, her voice almost drowned out by the storm, "Google Victor, Alexandra, and Elizabeth in Birmingham."

Henry typed and hit enter. Almost three million results. On the third page, beneath the glowing blue letters, Dr. Frank Williams was also listed. Henry clicked one more link, the page loading as thunder ripped through the house and the power died, leaving them in blackness.

The transformer shot sparks into the sky with an explosive roar and the streetlights went dark. William tried his high beams but they didn't penetrate very far into the pounding rain. The yellow line in the middle of the road was between his tires as he drove, fighting his way home. Through the storm, he could hear the sirens blaring their evacuation warnings, the sound mixing with the wind until it disappeared.

The car stalled as he pulled into Harrison Pointe, water flooding the engine. William turned the key, pounding his hand on the dashboard until the car roared back to life.

NOAA Alert: Hurricane Erika Potential Category 5; 150 Miles Southeast of Savannah, GA

Miami, FL—August 28, 2009, 7:13 PM: At 7 p.m. EDT, the National Hurricane Center is reporting that the center of Hurricane Erika is located about 150 miles southeast of Savannah, GA.

Erika is moving toward the west near 15 mph and this motion is expected to continue tonight and Saturday. On the projected path, the eye of Erika is expected to make landfall along the northern coast of Florida or the southern coast of Georgia late tonight.

Maximum sustained winds are near 150 mph with higher gusts. Erika is a potentially catastrophic Category 5 hurricane with some weakening in strength expected prior to landfall.

Hurricane force winds extend outward up to 50 miles from the center with tropical storm force winds for an additional 100 miles.

twenty seven

"We need to leave," Justine said, but she made no move to stand up.

The hissing of the wind came alive in the dark. Henry slid out of his chair and crawled beneath the desk to unplug the laptop from the docking station. Sitting on the floor, he tugged Justine's hand to pull her down next to him.

"This isn't good, Henry."

"I know."

The last page to load glowed on his laptop, running off the battery. "Without power there's no Internet," he said. "So, this is it."

His voice barely carried over the rain and wind, and the evacuation siren blared its ugly warning across the island.

On the verge of panic, William slid the car into the driveway, rolling up onto the grass. He jumped out, not even bothering to close the door as he ran up the steps, slipping in the rain and banging his knee into the wooden porch railing. The key wouldn't fit in the lock as his hands shook, and he tried to take a deep breath to still his fingers. Up and to the right, he jerked the knob but it didn't budge. Again, he fought to open the door.

Rain beat against him, and the wind howled in fury as the lock finally released. A branch broke off a tree, the sound echoing in the storm. The crack seemed to be right behind him and William stumbled against the door, pushing it open further. When he turned around to close it, lightning lit up the world. In the corner of his vision, he saw the shadow before anything else, long hair caught by the wind.

William opened the door wider. The rain flooded the floor until, with one more flash of lightning, the shadows were banished. The door broke halfway off its hinges with the blow as he staggered under the weight of his attacker. Long hair flew everywhere as he fell into the house and, with one final spike of lightning, William caught a single glimpse of the pipe right before it landed above his eyes.

The fury of the storm whistled up the stairs from the door, which banged open and closed downstairs. The wind seemed to be coming from all directions at once as Henry and Justine stared at the monitor.

Birmingham, AL—November 16, 2007: The bodies of Alexandra Raynes, 23, and her five-year-old daughter, Elizabeth, were discovered by Alexandra's parents, Douglas and Cynthia Raynes of Mountain Brook, late in the afternoon of November 14. The alleged shooter in the apparent murder-suicide, Elizabeth's father, Victor Steinlicht, 24, was rushed to Copper Green Hospital in critical condition.

"They'd just celebrated Beth's birthday," Cynthia Raynes said. "Everyone was there."

"That boy just destroyed our family," said Douglas Raynes. "Alexandra was just starting back at school, rest her soul."

A candlelight vigil is planned for the evening of November 16 at Mountain Brook Baptist Church on Montevallo Road.

Hospital sources, who wish to remain anonymous as they are not authorized to discuss the case, are now reporting that Steinlicht died late in the day on November 15, one day after shooting himself.

"He wasn't exactly a quiet boy-next-door type," said Police Sergeant Ralph Simson.

The office of Jefferson County Chief Medical Examiner Dr. Frank Williams released a short statement: "The body was cremated, per the wishes of the family."

Members of the Steinlicht family were unavailable for comment and messages left at their house were not returned.

The front door swung in the wind, knocking against the wall. In the flashes of lightning, William struggled to open his eyes, the pain of the first blow throbbing through his head. Above him, his attacker raised the pipe a second time. Thunder masked the hissing and the wind roared into the house with a vengeance. Each time he blinked, a double-image flashed across his vision, but the pipe obscured everything save for the long hair swirling around it as his sight faded away.

Shadows, confusing and out of focus, were everywhere as William fought to open his eyes again, waiting for the pipe to land one final time. A foot, indistinct in the darkness, stepped on his leg. Lightning, so close he could smell it, burned into his retinas until he couldn't see at all. Another foot stepped on his chest, trapping the air in his lungs. He tried to breathe, to twist away from the crushing weight, but only managed a weak cough, wet with blood.

Thunder shook the house and then the weight was gone as the shadows moved closer to the front door, seeming to struggle just to lift the pipe for another blow. William tried to move, crawling across the floor, dragging his unresponsive legs toward his bedroom. Behind him, his attacker fought to stand on the rain-soaked floor by the open door. The pipe slipped, flying out into the storm, and the shadows scrambled after the weapon, leaving William alone in the darkness in a growing pool of blood.

"Henry?" Justine said.

He pushed the laptop away; the picture of Alexandra, more achingly familiar than he wanted to admit, was bright in the dark room. The sirens blared and he stood up, pulling Justine with him. He shook his head. "We need to go," he said.

"They'll be evacuating over one bridge, Henry. It's going to be a parking lot."

"Call your parents."

She pulled the cell out of her purse, sliding it open. She turned it so he could see. "No service."

Rain pounded into his cheek and William opened his eyes. The front door was wide open but it was too dark to see. He tried to stand, slipping on the floor, his head spinning. When he wiped his hands across his face they came away covered in blood, deep red in the stark illumination of another lightning strike.

He pushed with his feet and slipped down the hall to his bedroom door, using the knob to pull himself up far enough to slide the key in the deadbolt. He collapsed to the floor again, vision swimming. He shook his head trying to clear it, but it didn't help.

On hands and knees, he crawled to the generator under the bed, hoping there was still gas in it. Over and over again, he pulled the starter until the humming filled the room. He dragged himself to the corner, pulling down the floor lamp by its cord until he could reach the button to turn it on. Light flooded the room and he looked back to the door. A long trail of blood covered the floor.

"Let's go," Henry said, pulling Justine toward him.

He carried his laptop, using the monitor as a flashlight to walk across the room and down the stairs. At the bottom, the floor was soaked from the rain and the door swung back and forth, unable to close. From his father's room, light filled the hallway that Henry rarely walked down.

They raced to the front door and Henry closed it, shoving his shoulder against the wood so the lock would turn. The sound of the sirens diminished but the screaming of the rain and wind continued.

"Dad?" Henry said, trying to scream louder than the storm as thunder shook the house again.

Together, they moved to where the tile changed to hardwood. At the end of the hallway, the door to his father's room swung ajar, light bleeding through the opening.

"Henry?" Justine said, her fingers moist in his as the blood streaks across the floor came into view.

At the door, Henry eased it farther open with his foot, not letting go of Justine's hand. In the far corner a floor lamp lay on its side, sending a cone of light into the wall. Odd shadows danced as the lamp rolled slowly back and forth. A twin mattress sat on the floor, squeezed against the wall, nothing but a thin quilt covering it.

"Oh," Justine said, her fingers squeezing hard enough to bruise although he couldn't feel the touch.

Banks of medical equipment glowed green and red around an empty hospital bed and multiple IV stands, tubes snaking down, attached to nothing. Leather restraints lay open on the mattress and a respirator sat dormant next to them. More equipment, lining the walls, came into view as the door opened fully.

"Dad!" Henry yelled as his father's body came into view, on the floor on the other side of the hospital bed. He dropped the laptop to the floor and worked his way around the room, stepping into a puddle of blood as he knelt next to his father. "Call 911!"

"No," his father said, his voice choked and weak. "No police."

Justine picked up the phone. "No dial tone."

"No police," his father said again.

"Why?" Henry asked. He checked his father's throat, unable to feel, with his numb fingers, how strong the pulse was. "Justine?"

She cradled his father's head in her lap, her fingers resting on his neck. Blood stained the front of his shirt and his face was bruised in the light from the medical equipment. Sirens continued outside and the front door crashed open once again in the wind.

"He needs a doctor," Justine said, her eyes white as she looked up.

"Get out," his father said. "Now, Henry."

"We're not leaving you. They're evacuating the island."

"No." The word was too soft to hear. "No."

"Dad!" Henry put his numb palms on either side of his father's face, turning him to look into his eyes. "We need to leave."

"I'm sorry, Henry."

"Let's go," he said, but no one moved.

His father's fingers fluttered weakly on his arm, scratching at the scar around his wrist. "I tried," his father said, the words ending in a cough, a thin trickle of blood leaking out of his mouth and down his chin.

"Dad?"

The front door slammed closed, cutting off the sirens. The hissing echoed down the hall as though the hurricane was stalking them.

"Get out!" his father pushed them away, rolling onto his side to point at the door. "Now!"

Justine took Henry's hand as the generator sputtered once and went still, plunging the room into darkness.

"The basement," Justine said.

Henry looked toward the bedroom door, where his father was struggling to stand before it.

"I don't think we can go that way," he said.

"I'm sorry," William said, using the floor lamp to get up, then holding it like an unwieldy sword and swinging it back and forth in front of the door.

A flash of lightning ripped across the sky, sending shadows around the room. Henry grabbed his father's arm but he pushed him away.

"Your mother"—his father's words caught on a series of coughs as the front door crashed open once again—"isn't very happy with me."

The sirens wailed through the house, carried on the wind and the rain as Hurricane Erika arrived on Saint Simons Island with a peal of thunder.

"I'm sorry," his father said. "She has nowhere else to go."

twenty-eight

XXX

Justine's hand in Henry's was far away, the storm farther still. Memories flickered on the edge of awareness but nothing was solid, nothing was real. He let her go and his fingers grasped the air, struggling to cling to a reality that was vaguely transparent.

Breathe.

The word was almost a silent hiss drowning in the storm.

Just breathe.

"Henry?" Justine cried out, shaking his arm.

He stood like a statue, unmoving.

"No," he said, the word a whisper. Then, again, "No."

His father took a step toward him, but Henry backed

away. "She died. In the accident." He wiped his fingers across his face. His hand came away covered in blood from his nose. "You told me—it was raining. You said there was an accident."

"Henry," his father said, his hand reaching toward his son.

"You told me she died."

The wind stormed across the island, a bitter roar slamming branches against the roof. Thunder shook the house as lightning sent shadows flashing around the room. The three of them stood there and no one said a word for a long moment.

"Henry," his father and Justine said at the same time.

He looked back and forth between the two of them, blinking, as tears fell down like rain.

"You died, Henry, not your mother." His father's voice was raw as he staggered against the floor lamp, the blood pooling at his feet.

"The cancer?" Justine asked, her voice breaking on the words.

William's eyes opened wide. "You know?"

Henry nodded.

"The cancer was killing you, yes."

"But?" Henry asked after too long of a silence.

"You died," his father said, taking another step toward him, "when I cut your head off."

"Save my son," Christine said, her dark hazel eyes almost green in the fluorescent kitchen lighting.

"He's my son too, Chrissy."

"I carried him," she said. "I raised him while you worked. Save my son!"

"How?" Frank put his coffee mug down untouched, then walked up to her but she turned away when he tried to put his arms around her. "What would you like me to do? The stem-cell transplant failed. It made things worse, for crying out loud."

"I don't care how, just save him. I can't stand by and watch him die and do nothing."

"I love you," he said, but if she heard, she gave no indication. "Chrissy?"

She looked up at him, a single glance before turning away.

"Have you talked to Dr. Saville?" he asked, the words as neutral as he could make them.

"About?" she said, then spun around to face him. "The fact that my son is dying? Everyone knows that, Frank."

"Your medication?"

"Please, like you'd notice if I took it or not." She rubbed her eyes, then pasted a smile on her face. "Like you care," she said, so quietly the words were no more than a hiss.

"Are you?"

"They made me sick," she said. "Well, sicker. I'd rather be me than nauseous."

He sat down, dropping his head in his hands and biting his tongue to keep quiet. Taking a deep breath, he looked back up at her. "There are other medications you can try, remember?"

"So I can force myself to be happy while my son dies, Frank? Is that the cure you want for me? No, I will not. Never. I'm sorry I can't be the happy little homemaker you thought you married." She laughed, a bitter sarcastic sound that lacked any trace of warmth. "Or do you still think we're the perfect family?"

He looked up at her, his breath short and hard as his heart tried to escape his body and break into little pieces.

"I love you."

"I know," she said, a smile just touching the edges of her chapped lips. "I've just forgotten why." The words hung in the air long after she ran from the room.

"What would you have me do, Chrissy?" he asked the emptiness. "What?"

She came out of nowhere, barreling into him, her fingers clenched into claws raking down his face. The tips came away bloody and her eyes, wide and red and staring, didn't even blink as she tried to catch her breath. A thin line of drool fell from her mouth to the floor. She snarled, then slammed her fist against the wall when he ducked her punch.

She gasped with the pain, then slid to the floor in a heap, her chest rising and falling faster than he could count. He reached a finger against her throat, trying to check her pulse, but she rolled away, kicking out at him.

"Save him," she said, her voice somewhere between a whisper and a moan. Then she screamed, the sound high-pitched

and painful. "Save my son!" She gulped air in between words, trying to catch her breath.

"How?" he said, trying to get his arms around her, to calm her, to hold her down. Her fingers clawed against his hands and the scratches on his face burned as she twisted around to try to bite him. She thrust her head back and up, into his chin, and he felt the rush of copper as he bit through his tongue.

Still, he wrestled her to the ground, forcing her down, her heart beating so strongly that he could feel it where his chest rested on her back. She shook beneath him and then released a harsh sob.

"Save my son," she said, more like a little girl asking Santa for a present than a grown woman talking to her husband. "Save him. Please, Frank. You can do that for me, right? You always said you'd do anything for me, to make me happy, to make me marry you. You said that. You promised."

"I'm sorry, Chrissy." His voice was quiet where he nestled his face in her hair. The usual sweet smell had been replaced by an acrid, sweaty odor, and dandruff flakes fell to the floor with her motions. "There's nothing I can do. The cancer's spread through most of his body. The stem-cell transplant was the last best hope."

"Then transplant something else," she said. Her voice, raw from screaming, still hissed out, like a child's doll talking. "If you love me, Frank, you'll save him. Transplant something else. Won't that work? You promised. Transplant everything—I don't care, just save my son!"

She beat her head against him again but he didn't feel

the blows, his eyes tearing as her words echoed in his head, his heart still within his chest.

He let her go and didn't even watch as she scrambled across the floor, crawling down the hall to Henry's room.

twenty nine

"Dr. Saville?" Henry asked, his voice little more than a whisper.

"Chrissy's doctor. Your mom told her, after the operation. She wanted to help but there was nothing she could do." His father looked around the room and his shoulders slumped.

"Victor." Henry said, the name strangely familiar when spoken out loud.

"Was dying. A suicide," his father said. "How do you know all this?"

"It wasn't easy." Justine closed the distance between herself and Henry, stretching out for his hand.

Her fingers were warm, and strength flowed through

her grip where they merged with his own. When he looked at her, she smiled, warm honey-brown eyes lit from within, glowing in the midst of the storm.

"It took months, practicing, studying, before I was ready," his father said. "I was so afraid you'd die before I found a donor match."

The storm shook the shutters, banging them against the house in a fury of wind and noise.

"Your mom wasn't well, Henry," he said. "Worried for you, not eating, not sleeping, but she pulled herself together enough to help me with you, to save you. We did it all for you."

The scalpel rested on the skin right above Victor's spinal cord and Frank looked at his wife. She smiled behind the mask, shifting the fabric. "Save our son," she said.

The blade sliced through the skin and the muscles beneath as he began the painstaking job of harvesting the head. A video camera feeding off the loupe view recorded every moment, software tagging the muscle groups, the individual veins and arteries.

Blood pooled down through the gurney to a series of tubes and into an automatic bucket brigade Frank had devised. The monitors were silent, muted, as the carotid was neatly sliced and Frank clipped a tag on the tie-off. On the screen, a flat green line scrolled by as machinery kicked into gear to keep the body alive.

Deeper, through the trachea, the esophagus, until only the spinal cord connected Victor to his head. The bone saw roared to life in the silence, slicing in one quick move through the vertebrae and their protected bundle of nerves.

Delicately, Frank lifted the separated head and placed it in a nutrient bath while Chrissy worked to stem the bleeding from the gaping wound, tying off the ends with loops of surgical tubing and pumps to prevent hypovolemia rather than cauterizing, in order to simplify the second phase of the surgery. The constant fear of decreased blood volume in the donor body was with him every step of the way.

In all, it had taken less than ten minutes to decapitate Victor.

A flip of a switch and anti-rejection meds joined the anesthesia flowing through the IV tubes.

Frank stripped off his bloody gloves, tossing them in the trash, and quickly regloved. He turned around to Henry.

The scalpel rested on his skin while Chrissy rushed over to place one last kiss on her son's forehead.

"Breathe," Frank said as he sliced through his son's neck. The second decapitation was quicker, routine, as the muscle groups curled back from the cut, the blood spurting in decreasing waves from the carotid as Frank sliced through Henry's spinal cord.

Blood dripped to the plastic sheeting over the carpeting as he carried his son's head as gently as he could to Victor's gurney.

With as much care and precision as he could manage, Frank sewed Henry's head on, beginning with the external and anterior jugular to get the blood flowing to Henry's brain, then following the template off the video feed in the corner of his glasses.

With his microscopic forceps and surgical tweezers, the sutures were as fine as medical science could provide. The nerves, impossible to sew, he welded, using surgical lasers to merge stem cells and create a perfect anastomosis between Henry's brain stem and Victor's spinal cord. Ventral ramus, vagus, phrenic, brachial plexus; the laser danced in his fingers until he clamped the artificial disc between C6 and C7 and moved on to the trachea a couple of hours later.

Around it all, he sewed the muscles back together until all that was left was the skin. The heavy line of stitches crawled across Henry's neck, then Frank wrapped bandages around the whole and allowed himself time to stretch.

Chrissy stood next to Henry's body, holding the lifeless hand, her eyes closed.

Frank pulled off his gloves, tossed them with the others, and checked the time. Two hours until dawn. A flip of a switch turned the volume back on, and Frank and Chrissy listened but there was nothing to hear, the flat green line on the monitor unbroken.

Frank pushed Chrissy out of the way and dragged the defibrillator to the side of the bed. "Clear," he said before touching the paddles to his son's chest. Henry's new body spasmed off the gurney, jumping at the hit of electricity. Still, the machines were silent.

"Clear!" Again, Henry's back arched up.

Frank closed his eyes and then re-charged the paddles. He was about to shock his son once more when the machines beeped. He listened to the beeping of Victor's heart, Henry's head resting between restraints to prevent movement, and began to cry.

"Well?" Chrissy asked, her fingers resting on her son's cheek.

Frank shrugged, unable to face her. "He's alive."

Henry's dad took another step closer, balancing with the lamp. His breath came in ragged gasps, and blood was still flowing from his scalp despite the towel he'd wrapped around it.

"And the rest of me?" Henry asked, the words forced out through clenched teeth as he waved his numb hand in front of his father's face.

"I couldn't figure out the dosages, the anti-rejection meds," his father said. "Parts of you started to die."

"Die?" Justine asked.

"I saved what I could, replaced what I couldn't." He closed his eyes. "I'm sorry."

Henry shook his head, his hair falling in front of his eyes. "No," he finally said. "We need to evacuate. We can talk later."

"It's too late," his father said.

"Why?"

"She couldn't live without you, Henry." His father sank to his knees, sliding down the lamp until he was kneeling in a pool of his own blood. Lightning flashed right outside the window and the thunder was right on top of them.

Hissing filled the room as the front door banged open in the wind. "I couldn't live without her."

"He's not going to wake up, is he?" she asked. Limp hair covered her face as her head rose and fell, pillowed on Henry's chest. Brittle fingers rested on her son's cheek, the cracked fingernails softly drumming on his skin.

"I don't know."

"You killed him," she said. "I watched you cut his head off."

"I'm still trying, Chrissy, please."

"I think," she said, brushing the hair out of her face so she could look up at him, "I don't..."

"Don't what?"

"Care." She closed her eyes, a smile spreading from ear to ear, exposing bloody gums.

"Chrissy?"

She opened her eyes but they were cloudy and distant, the smile still plastered on her face. Then she laughed, a harsh sound like a hiss as her fingers clenched around Henry's arm, the broken nails digging into his skin.

"Chrissy isn't here, please leave a message at the beep," she said, hissing again with every beep from the machinery attached to her son.

He closed the door behind him, leaving his wife snoring softly, a diseased smile across her prematurely aged face. Frank leaned back against the wall, closed his eyes, and cried. Great heaving sobs wracked his body and he pushed himself up, afraid he'd wake them with his cries. He stumbled to his office, falling into his chair and trying to will himself to sleep.

"Frank," Chrissy said, the words a million miles away in a dream of happier times; almost, he thought, a moan. "Frank." His name, so sweet on her supple lips; the honeymoon, the wedding itself. The dream wrapped him in a warm embrace.

"Frank."

He blinked, and saw a strange room, lit with computer diodes. He blinked again. His office snapped into focus.

She stood in the doorway, whispering his name.

"Frank."

Her skin was dark in the dim light, a glint of a reflection in her hand. The distant memory of a warm embrace … he looked down, caught the shadow lines of bloody handprints wrapped around his arms.

The chair fell over as he lunged to the light switch.

"Frank," she said again, as the glare reflected off the scalpel in her hand.

Blood pooled at her feet, dripping in a steady flow from her wrists. Beneath her chin, a hideous gash smiled at him, drooling blood.

"Frank."

She collapsed to the ground and he fell with her, trying to staunch the bleeding from her neck, her wrists, her beautiful face. Taking off his shirt, he wrapped it around her, tying it like a noose.

"Breathe," he said, but she was beyond breathing. "Don't leave me, Chrissy, please." He kissed her cheek, tasting her blood, unable to focus, rocking her in his arms, screaming her name.

Blood dripped between his fingers, staining the hard wood floor.

"Why, Chrissy?" he asked, his voice raw and strained.

"Save me," she said before drawing one last breath. And then she was still.

thirty

XXX

"There wasn't time to find a donor," his father said, still kneeling in a pool of blood.

"So you killed someone," Justine said, her voice flat and quiet.

"Her name was Sheila. I didn't even know if she was the right blood type."

"What went wrong?" Henry asked, taking the last step that separated him from his father. His feet squished in the blood as he knelt beside him.

"I rushed the transplant," his father said, "I was crying. I loved her; no, I love her. I cut her vocal cords with the scalpel. There was too much blood, and she'd already lost so much."

Henry rested his hand on his father's arm and William stared at the contact.

He took a deep breath, then looked up at his son and Justine. "For you, I'd stockpiled blood. I didn't have any for your mom except my own. I was so weak, and she was dying."

"You saved her," Henry said.

"She's not human anymore, Henry." His father closed his eyes. "I don't know what she is now. I'm sorry."

Henry pulled his hand away, breaking the fragile connection with his father. He opened his mouth to speak but no words came out. Lightning illuminated the room and he saw tears mixed with the blood on his father's face. Henry swallowed, struggling to remember the stranger standing next to him. "How did we end up here?" he asked in the silence after the thunder.

William opened his eyes, the faint memory of a smile crossing his face. "Dr. Saville grew up in this house, married some guy named Richard, but it didn't work out and she moved to Birmingham. When I needed a place to go, she gave me the keys." The smile grew enough to be seen for just a moment before fading away. "I moved us—the three of us. You were both in comas, unresponsive. I didn't know if the surgeries had worked, but you were both alive and too many people knew us in Birmingham. So we moved."

Faint sunlight filtered into the room through thick curtains drawn tight. The ceiling fan was still and the sound of the air-conditioning was drowned out by the hum of the machinery in the room. On the beds, Henry and Chrissy slept on.

The outside light faded as Frank's eyes fell closed, his last view that of his wife, sleeping peacefully.

The hiss was all around him. Air deflating a balloon, escaping a tire, moaning like wind scratching branches against a window trying to enter the room.

In his dream, a single hand reached off the bed to touch him, to hurt him. To pay back in kind.

Frank blinked. On the bed, Chrissy slept on, the monitors undisturbed. Her left arm, connected to the IV, rested at her side. Her right stretched out toward him. He stared, unable to move, afraid to breathe.

The fingers had uncurled, the entire arm hanging off the bed, the tip of her index finger almost, but not quite, touching his knee. Drawing in a breath, he stretched his hand out, preparing to move her arm back to the bed from where it had fallen. At his touch, her eyes screamed open, wide, frightened.

She hissed, the sound rough, forced through broken vocal cords. Her tongue slid out of her mouth as she rolled her head to the side and a strand of drool fell to the pillow.

"Chrissy!" He scrambled to the side of the bed, checking the monitors, but when he went to touch her, she hissed again. "Shhh," he said, raising his hand to caress her cheek.

She twisted off the thin mattress, crashing her teeth together hard enough to chip the enamel, straining to bite his fingers.

She thrashed on the bed, threatening to pull the IV out of her arm. Early morning sunlight poured into the room through cracks where the curtains met, a shaft of sunlight illuminating dust motes and falling on Henry's face. Frank tried to grab hold of Chrissy's arms, to keep her still, to keep her safe. She struggled against his touch, trying to reach her mouth around to bite him, and she kept attacking him each time she managed to free a hand.

He grabbed hold of her shoulders, his fingers sliding over the scar tissue on her neck, and she bent her head to try to bite him, twisting around. Then she was still, frigid and cold in his grasp, her muscles tight in his grip as she stared at her son.

She hissed, the sound somewhere between a moan and a name: "Henry." Though it was unrecognizable, Frank heard the name.

"Chrissy?" he asked, releasing the death grip he had on her arms.

With a spasm of her arm she smacked Frank across the chin, following up by biting his shoulder where it drifted too close to her mouth, the teeth puncturing the skin, drawing blood.

Dazed, he stumbled to the IV still taped into her arm and opened wide the morphine drip until her body slumped to the gurney. His blood dripped from her lips and gray hair was clenched in her fists where she'd pulled it out of his head.

"Henry," she whispered one final time, her eyelids fluttering, exposing crazed eyes. He placed her arms back on the bed before ransacking a closet of odds and ends in order to find leather cuffs to use as restraints.

Searching through his dwindling supplies, he mixed a cocktail of anesthesia, morphine, and benzodiazepine and hooked it up to her IV, sending her into a drug-induced coma.

Frank fell back into his chair, his shoulder bleeding through his shirt, thin trickles of blood sliding down from his scalp. More blood from his arms where her fingernails had raked through his skin.

It failed.

No.

I failed.

He couldn't kill her, not Chrissy, not the woman he'd fallen in love with, raised a son with. Not the woman he'd die for, that he'd killed for.

In a cabinet, he found another set of restraints and placed them on Henry's arms. He sighed, a tear sliding though one of the cuts on his face. The hospital bed scraped the door frame as Frank wheeled it out of the room, the equipment piled high on either side of Henry.

Through the empty kitchen there was a small laundry room, the windows looking out over a large backyard filled with trees. Frank pushed the bed up to the window, tilting Henry's face so that the sun landed on his skin.

"Welcome to Georgia, Henry," Frank said, squeezing the limp fingers in his hand. "Saint Simons Island. We live on an island, like we used to talk about, remember?" He wiped his sleeve across his eyes then looked at his son. "There's a big backyard. You'd have really loved it here, Henry."

Frank let go of his son's hand, pulled out a tissue, then blew his nose. "Hey, there's a squirrel out there too. And a bird feeder. Big trees. Magnolias, I think, big white flowers, and oak trees, draped in moss like in those pictures we used to look at."

Tears slid down his face and his nose was all stuffed up. "I'm sorry, Henry, I thought it would work." He sighed. "It should have, I guess. But, it didn't, not even close. All my fault. I failed. Twice."

He swallowed, trying to breathe, his eyes so raw it was difficult to focus as the sun warmed the small laundry room.

"I love you, Henry," he said. "I'm sorry."

Frank closed off the IV—cutting the nutrients, ending the morphine drip—and clicked the machines off. Not quite as dramatic as pulling the plug, but the end result would be the same. "I'm sorry," he said again, watching through his tears as the sun moved across the sky, leaving Henry's face in shadows.

In the semi-darkness it was difficult to see, the poor light playing tricks on his mind.

Henry drew in a deep breath, letting it out in a sigh.

He blinked. Again, and then turned his face away from the window. Machinery was piled up, surrounding him.

"Breathe, Henry," someone whispered. "Breathe."

"Who," he coughed again, his throat rough and raw, "is Henry?"

He fought to breathe, struggling to raise his hands. Someone pushed a button and the bed inclined, elevating him. Machinery slid down to the foot of the bed.

"Henry," the person said from the shadows at the foot of his bed. "Son, there was an accident."

NOAA Alert: Hurricane Erika Category 4; Landfall in Saint Mary, GA

Miami, FL—August 29, 2009, 12:43 AM: FOR EMERGENCY RELEASE:

At 12:17 a.m. EDT, Hurricane Erika made landfall in St. Mary's, Georgia; 31 miles north of Jacksonville, Florida, as a Category Four on the Saffir-Simpson Hurricane Scale with maximum sustained winds of 145 mph extending outward to sixty miles from the center and tropical storm force winds extending outward almost 150 miles.

Officials have reported successful evacuations of Amelia Island in Florida as well as Cumberland, Jekyll, St. Simons, and Sea Islands in Georgia.

St. Mary's, Georgia, in Camden County, population 14,000, is home to the Kings Bay Naval Submarine base.

thirty one

In the flashes of lightning, Henry caught glimpses of his father struggling to breathe. Justine's arms were warm around him, but he couldn't stop shivering. His father kept talking, struggling to stand up as words dripped out like individual drops of blood.

"When you woke up I called Dr. Saville," his father said. "She left Birmingham to try to help you but there was little she could do. Then, a few months ago, I woke Chrissy up. Thought I'd figured it out."

The hissing was everywhere, thunder and wind buffeting the house. Rain beat against the roof as though they lived under a waterfall.

"What?" Henry asked. "Figured out what?"

"Fix her." His father gasped, then closed his eyes, collapsing back to the floor as he turned his head to look at Henry. "Didn't…" he said. "Didn't work."

"Dad?"

"I kissed her. One last time." A tear fell, mixing with the blood. "Was going to end it, finally."

"Oh," Henry said, his hand falling to his side.

William took a deep breath, eyes wide and white in the darkness between lightning strikes. "She bit me. Broke free." He sighed, turned away. "I tried to find her. You have to believe me. I tried. Left food and medicine out for her, Henry. I tried."

Henry moved his hand forward to rest on his father's arm once again.

"Then what happened?" Justine asked.

"Murders. Started a couple days later. I don't know what she's doing any longer." He turned to face his son, fighting to stand up again. "I'm sorry."

Lightning threw shadows around the room. Outside, a shutter ripped off with the sound of breaking wood. The front door banged open in the wind. They heard it rip away, flying down the hallway to crash against the wall.

"Get out," William said. "Henry, go!"

"We're not leaving you."

Justine slid around him, reaching out a hand to help William stand, tugging on his sleeve.

Thunder rocked the house; for a moment, the hissing stopped. Then, louder than before, it was everywhere, crawling across their skin. Lightning strobed through the rain as the wind pressed in against them, shooting through the open front door.

"Find another way out," his father said, kicking with shaking legs to slam the bedroom door closed. "Just leave me here." He reached his hand up to his face, looking at the blood on his fingers. "I waited when I got home for her to come in from the storm. She attacked me."

"Dad."

The door to the bedroom crashed back open.

"She's here! Go!" William thrust himself out of their grip, standing on shaking legs between the doorway and them. He looked back at Henry. "Get out!"

He picked up the floor lamp and then pointed at the window, its broken shutters flapping like wings. "Now!"

"I love you," Henry said, but the storm drowned out the words.

William shook his head, then turned back to the door, wiping the blood out of his eyes so he could see.

The hissing came closer, carried on the wind, along with rain and leaves and branches freshly ripped off trees and still trailing Spanish moss. William swung the lamp around, threatening his balance.

Glass shattered as Henry battered at the window with the IV stand, clearing a space. Using the shaft, he broke out the jagged pieces from the bottom of the sill, then helped Justine through. Sharp edges cut her fingers and one of the shutters caught her side as she fell to the ground. Henry took one last look at his father then jumped through, breaking the remaining glass with his shoulder and landing hard on his side in a pile of broken branches.

Wind pounded them flat and the trees above them swayed beyond the tipping point, almost touching the ground. Rain hit hard enough to bruise, pounding into them. More branches whipped by, striking exposed skin and drawing thin trails of blood across their faces.

Henry scrambled to Justine, covering her with his body as the storm's fury washed over them. The remaining shutters beat against the house in time with the thunder.

Rain stormed through the house as William backed up against the wall, swinging the lamp in circles. Between flashes of lightning, Chrissy entered the room, hair flying around her face in the wind.

"Henry?" she asked, the name nothing more than a hiss.

William held the lamp in front of him, the point dipping toward the ground as he ran out of strength to hold it up. In the shadows, he held his arms out to his wife.

"Chrissy." Blood dripped into his eyes and he swayed with the wind, too weak to fight the pressure of the storm. "I love you."

His knees buckled, dropping him to the floor as the lamp clattered away.

thirty two

XXX

"We have to go!" Henry screamed into Justine's ear, the words torn from his mouth by the wind.

Lightning strikes sliced through the night, the thunder rolling in waves over them. The wind carried ozone and sea salt along with the leaves and debris flying past them.

Justine nodded beneath him.

"You okay?" he asked.

Again, she nodded. If she spoke, he couldn't hear the words.

He squeezed her shoulder, kissed her head beneath him, and fought to stand up in the wind. He braced his feet to stop his slide across the leaf-strewn wet grass and held tightly to her hand. Together they bent over, running close to the ground around to the front of Henry's house. On the side, the wind lessened, blocked partially by Justine's home standing tall, dark, and empty above them, and then they were past it, running toward the street.

Gusts blew across the road and a stop sign skittered along the pavement, tumbling end over end. Soaked to the skin, weighed down by their clothes, they ran up the street.

"Henry!"

He looked over at Justine, the tails of her shirt whipping behind her. Hair lay plastered on her face and tiny drops of blood beaded on her arms before being washed away in the rain.

"Where?" She screamed the word, pointing to the intersection in front of them. Water lapped at the edges of the road, almost up to their ankles. Both ways, there was nothing to see. No lights in any direction. Just water, broken trees, and downed power lines dangling into the flood, thankfully not carrying electricity.

The wind battered them and Henry wrapped his arms around her. "We can't go that way!" he said, straining to be heard.

She stretched up to his ear. "I know!"

"Where?"

"My purse," she said.

"What?"

"It's in your house, with my key."

"Your house?" he asked.

"Key!"

"Break in?"

"Yes!" she screamed in his ear, then grabbed his hand again.

They ran with the wind now, blowing them down with each gust. Their clothing was torn, soaked with rain and blood. A branch came out of nowhere and clipped Henry across his right arm; he didn't feel it though it knocked him off balance, sending him crashing to the street. Justine's fingers slipped out of his hand as he fell.

"Henry!" she screamed, running back for him. She pulled him up, fighting the wind. When he put weight on his legs, he collapsed back to the ground.

Lightning lit up the world. It illuminated a figure at the end of the street, standing in the water, long hair whipping around in the wind. Then the light disappeared, taking the person with it. The after-image, a shadow standing there against the wind, stayed with them every time they blinked.

"Was that your mom?" she yelled in his ear.

He shrugged and scrambled to his feet, limping as they continued running. Another shutter tore free from his house, slamming into the wall like a gunshot before flying through the air to land behind them.

Wind stung their eyes and the rain beat on their unprotected heads as they ran up Justine's steps. Henry slammed his shoulder into the door but it wouldn't budge, and he caught his forehead on the brass doorknocker.

Justine looked around the porch, then picked up a small planter; the petals had been stripped from the flower and the bare green stalk stood defiantly against the wind.

Turning around, she threw it into the boards that her father had nailed up over the living room window. Again, she pounded against the same spot until the wood finally splintered.

Together, they clawed at the board with their fingers, prying the hole wider until they could see the glass behind it.

The heavy rain came down sideways and wind pushed the matching pair of rocking chairs crashing to the railing of the porch.

"Faster!" Justine screamed. They reached through the small hole and pulled despite the splinters, forcing the nails slowly out of the siding.

The plywood came loose with a snap, falling on top of them, and the storm flipped it end over end toward the street. Justine picked the planter back up and threw it against the window. Glass shattered into the house, caught on the wind.

"Hurry!" Justine said as she jumped, breaking through the remaining glass. A shard stabbed into her leg and she screamed, tumbling to the floor as the piece of glass stuck out of her thigh. Henry jumped after her and spikes of glass at the bottom of the sill cut through his pants. The screaming of the storm lessened once they were inside, even though the wind and rain followed them through the broken window.

Justine crawled across the floor holding her thigh, glass cutting into her palms.

Henry slid to the floor next to her, slicing open his knees, and wrapped his arms around her.

She looked at him, teeth gritted against the pain. "Pull it out."

"Ready?" Henry asked, his fingers slipping against the sides of the glass.

"Do it."

Wind whistled through the broken window and rain pooled on the floor around them. Henry pulled off his belt and tied it around her leg.

"Now," he said and she squeezed her fingers down on his foot as he pulled the glass out.

Blood soaked through her clothes. Henry tightened the belt and pressed his hands into her thigh until the bleeding stopped. When he looked up, her face was pale, eyes wide open in a sea of tears.

"You all right?" he asked.

Justine smiled, then a harsh little laugh escaped. "No," she said, and then laughed again.

Lightning flashed and the thunder followed immediately behind. A shadow fell across the window, but it was difficult to see once the lightning went away.

"Get up!" Henry screamed, reaching for Justine's hand.

He wrapped his arm around her and she leaned against him as they scrambled to the kitchen, both limping.

"On the counter," she said, pointing to the knife block next to the sink.

Henry and Justine backed up until they had no place else to run. Knives in each hand, they waited in the kitchen.

thirty three

XXX

Lightning struck a tree outside, sparks shooting off as the top half broke free, crashing into the roof. Plaster fell from the ceiling, sticking to their skin, wet with rain and blood. A figure appeared in the doorway, long hair dripping water to the floor.

"Mom?" Henry said, his voice raw. He lowered the knives.

Another lightning strike, and the shadows disappeared.

Long hair flying in the wind, a sick grin missing a tooth, and unmistakably male.

William took a shallow breath, then fought his eyes open. Lightning lit the room, the wind whistling through the broken window. Chrissy sat with him, his head in her lap as her fingers played through his hair. Her every breath came out as a hiss, forced through what remained of her throat.

"Henry?" she whispered.

William blinked, but she was still there, the faint trace of a smile somewhere in her damaged face. "Chrissy." He coughed, trying to clear his lungs. A bubble of blood popped as his lips opened. "What happened?"

"Henry?" she asked again.

"Storm," he said, pointing toward the window. "Thought you were chasing them."

Her eyes widened and she shook her head. She moved him to the floor and ran to where the broken glass was letting the hurricane in.

"You attacked me." He stretched out toward her but she was too far away. His arms fell to the ground.

At the window, she shook her head again.

"Chrissy," he said, then louder to be heard over the wind. "Chrissy!"

She turned around and looked at him. "Henry?"

"You didn't?" he asked, pointing to his head, where the blood still ran in thick rivers down his skin.

Once more, she shook her head.

His eyes closed as another cough sent dizzy waves of nausea through him.

"Henry?"

William sighed. "I don't know," he closed his eyes. "I thought it was you."

Lightning broke the sky open, slicing through the tree outside.

"I'm sorry," he tried to say, but by the time she reached her husband's side, he was beyond speaking.

"Frank," she said, the word barely more than a sigh, impossible to understand, and then she kissed him one final time as he died.

The stranger hissed, raising a pipe over his head, swinging it at random in the darkness as he walked toward them.

"Justine, run!" Henry screamed, standing between her and the stranger, knives held high in front of him once again as the footsteps came closer.

Glass shattered to the floor from the kitchen door, and another body crashed into the man with the pipe. Rain poured into the room, the wind screaming across them. Justine grabbed Henry's hand as the two people rolled over each other on the floor.

The man landed on top, raising the pipe high as he prepared to strike. As one, Henry and Justine lunged forward, each driving a knife into his side. The pipe fell out of his hand as he toppled to the ground.

Lightning struck again, lighting the room. Beneath the dying man, a woman struggled to free herself.

Henry pulled the body off and the woman scrambled

back against the wall. Long brown hair lay flat against her scalp, and even in the dim light he could see the necklace of scars she wore.

"Henry," she hissed, almost a moan, the word barely recognizable.

"Mom?"

Hope and Tragedy in the Aftermath of Erika

Saint Simons Island, GA—August 31, 2009: Over three thousand Glynn County homes are still without electricity two days after Hurricane Erika made landfall to the south, in St. Marys, before turning north inland to Atlanta. It will be the end of the week before full power is restored, utilities management has said. The U.S. Department of Energy, concentrating most resources in Camden County, which suffered a direct hit, says that power has already been restored to 38 percent of those residences in Georgia that lost power in the storm.

Mayor Jim Monroe of Brunswick, helping local businesses clean up the island, praised the efforts of law enforcement and the citizens of Glynn County. "The Golden Isles should be incredibly proud of the men and women who serve here."

Damage estimates range into the tens of millions, but thanks to the efficient evacuation of the islands, the human toll was remarkably low. "A couple of fender benders and minor accidents," said police spokesperson Carmella Rawls. "The tragic death of local resident William Franks, who died during the storm, has led to the successful resolution of the vicious murders which have plagued Glynn County this summer."

"Blunt force trauma," said Major Daniel Johnson at a hastily called press conference in the aftermath of the storm. "Mr. Franks is the final victim of Richard Adims."

Adims, 41, a former resident of Waycross, had been institutionalized at Georgia Regional Psychiatric Hospital after being found unable to stand trial for a series of beatings due to mental incompetence. In May, Adims was transferred to Turning Point Hospital after biting off a part of his tongue in an apparent suicide attempt. After attacking a guard on the transport, Adims escaped and had been on the loose ever since.

Dr. Jason Rapp, Chief of Staff at the GRPH, released a brief statement to the press: "Due to a computer error, Richard Adims was mistakenly classified as an N-VO, Non-Violent Offender. In the confusion after the unfortunate situation earlier this year concerning the supervision of patients, this misclassification went unrectified. Funds have been requested from the State discretionary account to assure this does not happen again."

Repeated calls to the Georgia Regional Psychiatric Hospital for additional information went unreturned.

The body of Richard Adims was found in the debris after the storm in a subdivision on St. Simons Island. The alleged cause of death is puncture wounds that police spokesperson Carmella Rawls says Franks was able to inflict upon his assailant.

"It appears that the suspect, Richard Adims, intended to seek shelter with relatives, who, unfortunately for William Franks, live next door to the Franks' residence on St. Simons. But Mr. Adims went to the Franks residence instead, where he once lived with his first wife, Margaret Saville, a local psychologist. In the struggle," Ms. Rawls said, "Mr. Franks suffered a severe blow to the head from the pipe that allegedly was used by the suspect in previous attacks. In self defense, the victim was able to fatally wound his assailant."

"The people of Glynn County and the Golden Isles are eternally grateful for all of the hard work and dedication of FLETC, the various police departments, and the many people who gave of their time to aid us this summer," said Mayor Monroe.

William Franks is survived by one son, Henry, 16.

thirty four

XXX

The funeral was larger than he'd expected. Police officers coming to pay their respects, a sizable contingent of journalists following behind local politicians, and numerous strangers coming together as a community after the storm. Relatives of other victims attended; most left without saying a word but some approached, resting a hand on the casket or offering Henry a tentative hug.

He stood with Justine and her parents as William Franks was laid to rest. Bandages still covered Justine's arms, but her fingers were soft and warm and never far away.

As the casket sank into the welcoming earth, Henry looked around, shading his eyes from the sun. September's heat burned down, erasing the memories of the storm despite the broken trees and the blue tarps covering homes that had lost roofs. In the distance, a lone woman leaned against a grave until long after the other mourners had left.

They found her sitting in the freshly turned dirt, facing the space where a tombstone would be someday. The sun was low in the west and his elongated shadow fell across her as Justine's fingers slipped out of his hand.

A twig or two was caught in her hair, the dirty brown strands hanging limply against her shoulders as she rocked back and forth on the ground.

"Mom?" he said, the word soft and quiet in the stillness of the empty cemetery.

Her rocking stopped and her head jerked up. The scar around her neck caught the fading sunlight as she turned to look at him. A smile spread across her face and her eyes, almost a match of his own, glistened, but try as he might, he couldn't remember anything more than what the photos in his scrapbook told him.

"Henry," she said, the word broken and harsh.

Next to him, Justine wrapped her fingers around his arm and gently pushed him forward. He stumbled with the first step, then ran to close the distance. Christine's arms, wrapped protectively around him, held him in a fierce hug as she whispered his name into his hair.

His mother lifted her head to look at him as the sun set behind them. She rested dirty fingers on either side of his face and smiled. Releasing him, she reached an arm out to Justine and pulled her closer, placing Henry's hand into Justine's with another smile.

"Henry," his mother said.

Through his tears, he watched as the moon lit her face. She touched the dirt and looked back at Henry. "I'm sorry," she said, mouthing the words since few sounds would come through her damaged vocal cords.

From behind the fall of his hair, he studied her face, the pale skin and its necklace of scars.

"Remember me," his mother whispered before dropping to the ground.

"Mom!" Henry said, but she was beyond hearing him. He pulled her up to rest against his shoulder and brushed his hands through her tangled hair. Blood dripped from his nose to land in the dirt of the grave as his mother died in his arms.

In his bedroom, he flipped through the scrapbook without speaking; one picture of his mother, smiling as she looked at him, kept his attention.

"I'm sorry," Justine said.

"Not your fault."

"You always say that." She took his hand. A single photograph, of Henry caught between his parents. On the monitor, another picture, of Henry gaunt and losing his battle with cancer.

"When will you leave?" she asked.

"For Birmingham?"

She nodded but didn't speak.

"Someone from Children's Services stopped by. Not really sure what's going to happen. Besides, what would I say? What would I do? I don't remember anyone."

"You have friends there," Justine said.

"I have you, here." He looked at her and ran his finger down her cheek. A tiny scar was all the evidence remaining on her face of the storm. "I'd rather stay."

"Henry."

"Justine," he said before kissing her, wrapping his arms around her and holding tight. He broke the kiss and looked down at her, so close he could feel her breath warm on his skin. "I'm dying."

She tried to push him away but he wouldn't let her go.

"Again," he said, soft and gentle.

"No."

"Yes."

"Why?" she asked.

"The pills. Look." He pointed his chin at the desk. A plastic tray rested next to his laptop; over half the compartments were empty.

"Get more," she said.

"I can't. My father made them. He mixed them himself."

"Henry."

"I tore his room apart, trying to find notes, but there was nothing. He must have gotten rid of everything with those old photographs. I'm sorry."

"Stop saying that." She squeezed her eyes shut, clutching her fists into his shirt, burying her head into his shoulder.

He could feel her tears soaking through the fabric. She sobbed against him and he rubbed her back, pulling her still closer.

"When?" she said.

He shrugged against her. "Soon? I don't know. Eventually, my body will reject the transplants. I think that's what happened to my mother."

"You're still you, Henry," Justine said.

"Am I?" he asked, running a hand through his hair so that it was no longer covering his eyes. "Which part of me is me?"

She kissed him, once, short and fierce. "Did you feel that?"

Henry nodded.

Justine ran her fingers across his face. "Feel that?" she said, so quietly the words were little more than a breath in his ear.

"Yes."

"Don't give up," she said. "Don't you dare. There are doctors; they'll help you."

"What can I tell them?" he asked. "'My father put my head on someone else's body'? Even I don't believe that and it happened to me."

"Tell them anything," she said. "Tell them nothing or everything or something in between. Just try. Please, for me, try."

He nodded.

"You could give them the pills—can't they analyze them or something?"

"You talk too much, you know that?" he said, brushing a kiss across her forehead.

"I'm sorry." Justine smiled, then lifted her lips to his.

epilogue

XXX

Justine Franks, MD, FACS
St. Simons Island, Glynn County, GA
Tuesday, December 21, 2027
Patient X

Patient presents with systemic organ failure due to general transplant rejection. Past history suggests patient has developed immunity to all but toxic levels of immunosuppressants and nanotech-based anti-rejection medications. Research continues in conjunction with the Emory University Transplant Center into the effects of the Franks laser weld on the regeneration of spinal stem cells, but the prognosis for

Patient X remains constant: complete failure of all transplanted systems imminent.

Prescription at this time is to continue IV Interferon therapy in overdose quantities as well as gluccocorticoids; opioids, as needed, for pain management. Patient has been entered into rotation for current drug testing trials for bio-engineered nanotech and gene therapy that has shown promise in early stage animal experimentation, but the prognosis is unchanged.

Justine pushed herself back from the desk and put her tablet to sleep. The screen flickered once and went dark. She rubbed her eyes, took a deep breath, and dropped her head back, staring at the ceiling.

"Lights," she said. The LEDs dimmed, leaving sunlight alone to illuminate her office. Shadows from the trees outside the window crawled across the room. With a heavy breath, she stood up and stretched.

Across the hall, Justine put scrubs on over her clothes, then washed her hands and arms in the stainless steel sink before applying disinfectant and gloving up. Outside the bathroom, she stepped into self-sealing surgical booties on the hardwood floor. From windows high up the walls, sunlight filtering through the Spanish moss lit up the air.

The master bedroom door still had the deadbolt lock, but it opened at a touch of her elbow on the sensor next to the knob. Inside, the curtains had been left open, filling the room with December warmth from the Georgia sun. Justine absorbed the data from the bank of machines lining the walls with just a look.

On the bed, Patient X could barely be seen, buried beneath a mass of IV tubes snaking into each arm and leads to the electronic monitors. An implanted defibrillator was the only wireless device in the room; nothing was allowed to interfere with its activities.

As she reached the bed, his eyes opened.

"Hi," she said, resting the back of her hand on his forehead before letting her fingers trail down his face. "Need to shave you again."

"I thought—" He coughed, his frail body shaking in the bed. "I thought you liked the beard?"

"Mary says it itches," she said with a smile. "Me too."

"Makes her sneeze." He shrugged. "Then she laughs."

"Speaking of Mary," Justine said, "I thought she was in here with you."

"Just left," he said, then coughed again. "Sorry."

"Feeling any better today?"

"Yes," he said, shaking his head to lessen the meaning. "Maybe?"

She leaned down, resting her face against his cheek. Her voice was soft in his ear. "I love you, Henry."

Farther down the hospital bed, his fingers fluttered in vain, trying to rise up far enough to stroke her hair, to hold her close. With a harsh sigh of frustration, he dropped his hand back to the bed, hardly having moved it at all.

"I love you too," he said.

When she looked at him, his eyes were closed, a single tear hanging on one of his few remaining eyelashes. A trail of blood ran from his nose to his lips, the color stark red on his pale skin.

"Your nose is bleeding," she said, wiping his face with a tissue.

"It's the medicine." He laughed, once, the sound weak and faint. "They give me nightmares, too."

"Liar," she said. "They do not." She smiled, and then kissed him. When the kiss ended, she gave him a long look, studying his face. "Though, yes, they do sometimes give you nosebleeds still. I'm working on that."

"Anything you're not working on?" he asked.

She pushed herself up until she was leaning over him. Her smile was gone and her warm honey eyes were determined. "I couldn't save your mother, Henry. I can save you."

"You already did."

She shook her head, sending a lock of hair flying out of the surgical cap.

"Yes, you did, Justine," he said. "When you married me, when you gave birth to our daughter; you saved me."

Her tears splashed onto his face as she kissed him. Again, his fingers fought to rise up and she stopped the kiss to reach back and pull his arms around her.

"Mary needs her father," she said. "I need you."

He smiled. "I'm here."

"You're dying," she said, wiping the tears off her face with the sleeve of her gown.

"I've died before," he said with a hollow laugh.

Justine slid her fingers down to his until they were holding hands, the IV tubes twisted around them.

Outside the window, the sun slowly disappeared into the marshes. Long shadows of skeletal trees stretched across the bed. Stirred by the wind, a branch skated across the window. The sound, almost a hiss, was drowned out by the softness of her breathing in his ear as she lay down next to him.

"Henry," she said, her voice welcoming and warm. "I can save you."

From the edge of sleep, he forced his eyes back open. "How?" he asked.

"We just need to find another donor."

Acknowledgments

This book would not exist at all if not for the assistance and support of so many people who were always there to answer random questions, or read out-of-context chapters, or, really, just always there for me. I will try not to leave anyone out of these thank you's!

As I struggled to write convincingly of medical and psychological processes, much is owed to Dr. David Alexander and Dr. Robert Bachner. Any errors are mine alone.

Special thanks to my wonderful alpha reader and editor, Terri Molina (a fantastic author well worth looking up), as well as my beta readers: Meg Stocks, Jon Cohen, and Staci Carson. Also, I would be remiss if I didn't mention two other early readers who read numerous versions of this book and never wavered in their encouragement, enthusiasm, and very constructive criticism: My uncle Ken Salomon and my sister's mother-in-law (yes, really) Elaine Steinfeld.

This writing career of mine simply would never have been possible without the steadfast support of my parents, Robert and Claudia Salomon, and my sister Shayna Steinfeld (as well as her husband, Bruce, and my nephews Justin, Zachary, and Dylan).

Most of all, so much is owed to the encouragement and support of my wife and children! Thank you so much, for everything. I love you more than words.

I also want to recognize Darin and Kate Martin for web and computer support above and beyond the bonds of family (and to thank Kate for blessing me with her daughter's hand in marriage). To Jillian Boehme: you helped start this ball rolling down the hill and I wish you the greatest success. You do a great good in this world. And to Jeannie Mobley, fellow debut author, who has unlimited karma on the way.

To my wonderful agent, Ammi-Joan Paquette: thank you, thank you, a thousand times thank you. Thank you as well, of course, to my editor, Brian Farrey-Latz! To the Gango and the EMU's Debuts, thank you for the never-ending support, encouragement, and incredible capacity for putting up with my personal brand of insanity. To Authoress and the rest of the Miss Snark's First Victim community (and Success Stories): Never stop helping others learn that dreams come true!

Finally, I write because of my grandfather, Andre Scara Bialolenki. I am following his legacy with every word. He brought harmony to the world and I am forever grateful for everything he shared with me. I wrote a poem for him the day he died and read it in the rain at his funeral. One line is worth sharing as I acknowledge his contribution to my life and this book: "He was composer and conductor/finding symphonies and poetry/where others heard only silence." He taught me how to listen. I spoke of him when I first announced that this book would be published and always promised myself that my first novel would be dedicated to him.

Grandad, thank you, I love you, I miss you. This book is for you.

About the Author

Peter Adam Salomon lives in Chapel Hill, North Carolina, with his wife and three sons. *Henry Franks* is his debut novel.

For more information, visit www.peteradamsalomon.com and www.henry-franks.com.